A WEEK IN TURENEVO

and Other Stories by

Alexei Tolstoy

Introduction by George Reavey

GROVE PRESS, Inc.
New York

A Week in Turenevo is published in three editions:
  An Evergreen Book (E-89)
  A hard bound edition
  A specially bound, Limited Edition of 100 numbered copies

Grove Press Books and Evergreen Books
are published by Barney Rosset at Grove Press, Inc.
795 Broadway   New York 3, N. Y.

MANUFACTURED IN THE UNITED STATES OF AMERICA

CONTENTS

INTRODUCTION

by George Reavey

1

Alexey Nicolaievich Tolstoy was born in 1882 on an estate near Sosnovka, a village in the steppe region of the Province of Samara. This region lay on the Eastern or Asiatic side of the mighty Volga which has figured so often in legend and folk-song. Through Samara, the capital of the Province, which has been renamed Kuibyshev in Soviet days, had passed from olden times Novgorod merchants and Moscow Princes, English adventurers in search of a trade route to Persia and India, conquering Mongols, Tartar hordes and the armies of Muscovy. Samara had known, too, the pirate flotillas of Stenka Razin, the terrors of the Pugatchev rebellion and, closer to our day, the alarms and sufferings of the civil war and the consequent famine. It was a city that Alexey Tolstoy knew well: a city on the borders of the Asiatic steppes and the Kirghiz deserts, a trading post for camel caravans and Volga port. It was a city of rich merchants and dockers, bargees and "boatmen," a city of rough exuberance and tough, if not madcap, behaviour. Samara was notorious not only for the "shoving and shouldering" of its barges, but also for the "three day orgies of the successful merchant and the celebrating local landowner. But, apart from the impressive Volga scenery on the Western side, of sanded bank, forest, and wild hills, it was by all accounts as dull as most of those Russian provincial towns, which have been so caustically described by writers ever since the days of Pushkin and Gogol. It was the sort of town that Gogol's Chichikov might have passed through in quest of "dead souls." In 1941-43, as the slightly more industrialized Kuibyshev, it had served as a haven for the Diplo-

matic Corps; and its provincial tedium was then somewhat
relieved by the presence of the Moscow Bolshoy Theatre
Opera and Ballet.

Alexey Tolstoy did not emerge from the "people" or the
"lower depths" as did two other notable artists of the Volga
region—Fyodor Chalyapin and Maxim Gorky. Nor did he
come from the merchant class or the intelligentzia. He came,
like the previous generations of great Russian writers, from
the landed gentry. On his father's side, Count Alexey Tolstoy
was descended from one of the branches of that Tolstoy family,
which had already been politically active in the reigns of Boris
Godunov and Peter the Great. In the nineteenth century, the
Tolstoys had given Russia two famous writers: Leo Tolstoy
and A. K. Tolstoy. Count A. K. Tolstoy (1817-70), the historical novelist and dramatist, is less well known in Europe and
America than the author of *War and Peace;* but his dramatic
trilogy, *The Death of Ivan the Terrible, Tsar Feodor,* and *Tsar
Boris,* is still often performed by the Moscow Art Theatre.
Thus, Alexey Tolstoy is the third of that branching family to
have made a name for himself in Russian literature. We must
note, too, that his mother was a Turgenev; and, as we know,
in his youth he steeped himself in Turgenev's novels.

Alexey Tolstoy, therefore, had behind him the tradition of
the landed gentry and, in literature, the novel of the manor
house. The preoccupations and the cerebrations of the city
intelligentzia were originally alien to him as was also the
display of any social or political ideas and attitudes. Later in
Petersburg, it is true, he became enveloped in an intellectual
atmosphere, but the envelope always remained thin and dis-
pensable. When he treats of the "intellectual," Alexey Tolstoy
cannot avoid a note of ironic detachment as in his story, *The
Man in Pince-nez.* As a writer, Alexey Tolstoy, despite his
many bypaths, remains rooted on the whole in his gentry background and in the historical past.

2

2

The Petersburg of 1907, where Alexey Tolstoy began his literary apprenticeship, was still digesting the effects of the 1905 Revolution and the repressions that followed it. The more militant voices were muted: Maxim Gorky had been in exile since 1906. The scene was dominated by the poets, symbolists, mystics and aesthetes. The poetic revival, which in the 1890's under the banner of Symbolism had succeeded the great age of prose, was now in full swing; and the lyrics of Bryusov, Blok, Biely, Vyatchislav Ivanov, had introduced a new note of musicality, refinement and, in some cases, abstract detachment. At the same time, Andrey Biely's contrapuntal effects and his use of the word as "symbol" were adding new dimensions to the world of prose. It was the period, too, of Diaghilev and the *World of Art*. The more socially-minded writers were out of fashion. But even among the Symbolists there were differing attitudes: while Ivanov continued to inhabit his "Ivory Tower," Blok and Biely in their different ways came to grapple with a larger reality in symbolical terms; and no writer better than Biely in his intense and nervous lines succeeds in conveying to us the sense of the abyss underlying the frail superstructure of everyday life.

Alexey Tolstoy met the Petersburg poets, aesthetes and bohemians, and absorbed some of that rare atmosphere which was so different from his Samara background. His first literary venture was a book of poems, *Lyrics* (1908), which reflected his association with Vyatcheslav Ivanov and the poets of the "Ivory Tower." Next year he published a book of folk tales and then, in 1911, his second and last collection of poetry, *Beyond Blue Rivers,* in which he turned to mythology, folklore and the world of pagan Slavs.

In 1909 Alexey Tolstoy had already begun to concentrate on the short story and the novel. He had indeed written prose since 1902, but from now on he was to make it his chief medium. Gradually he was to eliminate the aesthetic mannerisms and to perfect a more robust and realistic style of his own based on the racy language and the rhythm of his native province. Before 1914, Alexey Tolstoy was already regarded by critics a leading representative, together with Prishvin, Zaitzev and Zamyatin, of a new neo-realistic trend in Russian prose—a trend that cut across both the "symbolic" and the "social" prose. About this time, Alexey Tolstoy published in a review, *Behind the Stage,* a statement of his artistic views, an exerpt from which reads: "Since the forties Russian literature had assumed the burdensome and far too exacting task of fighting for civil liberty, for external liberty, whereas art is essentially concerned with internal freedom, the illumination of the spirit, the emergence of man from chaos into the light of the eternal sun. In the name of humanity, Russian literature had turned its back on these goals which are alone its sphere of activity." This was, of course, a criticism of any involvement on the part of a writer in politics or social programs and it was naturally bound to displease the revolutionary democrats, but it did not adversely affect Tolstoy's rising reputation as a writer. Indeed, ever since he published his first book of stories in 1910, he commanded a larger and more appreciative public; and within a year he was no longer an apprentice. By 1911, his course as a short-story writer and a novelist was fully determined; and as such we must appreciate or judge him.

With the War of 1914, not unnaturally, another element began to intrude into Alexey Tolstoy's work; the feeling for the past, the unity of his old world characters, so typical of his pre-war stories and novels, tends to be broken up and his work becomes shorter and less sustained. *Rastegin's Adventures* (1913-15) a boisterously written short novel about the strange escapades of a rich merchant and his involvement with an incalculable girl, which created a sensation at the time, was still a transition piece in older vein. But, by 1916, his job as a war correspondent involved him in current journalism and made him turn to war themes and incidents in such stories as *Submarine* or *The Fine Lady,* which are sketchier and less compelling than his earlier stories. However, in a longer story

4

written at this time and having nothing to do with the war theme, *The Man in Pince-nez,* Tolstoy gives us a more subtle, though ironic portrait of a frustrated intellectual whom the illusion of love wakens for a moment out of his torpor. This state of torpor or dream-state is characteristic of many of Tolstoy's personages: they seem to live in a hermetic, semi-conscious world of their own (like David Davydovich in *The Ravines)* until they are briefly jolted out of it by outside interference only to sink back again into lethargy or be destroyed unless they are rescued and, in some way, transformed by the magic medications of love.

The war years showed that Alexey Tolstoy was never quite himself when facing the more immediate reality of the times: his talent seemed to require the stimulus of that more familiar background which was rooted in the traditions of his gentry past, folklore, local tradition or history. He was happiest, perhaps, and also at his best in a sort of blend of the actual and the traditional, of his own observation and the historical anecdote. As we shall see, he also eventually turned out to be, in his *Peter the Great,* a first rate historical novelist.

3

The October Revolution, the Civil War, and the Allied Intervention, all brought about a situation in which Russian writers had to choose between staying at home or flying abroad. Alexey Tolstoy actually sided with the "Whites" and, in 1919, emigrated *via* Odessa to France, where he lived and worked until 1921. In that year, under the influence of the *Change-of-Landmarks* movement which sought to find a basis of agreement with the Bolsheviks, Alexey Tolstoy swung over to the acceptance of the revolutionary regime as a Russian *national* phenomenon. He came to Berlin and, after some preparatory writing display of his "reliability," was admitted back, in 1922, to the land of his ancestors which, in any case, as some of his own earlier stories, like *Arkhip,* had exemplified, had never been quite a safe place for the gentry. However, unlike Leo Tolstoy, Alexey Tolstoy was no moralist, no ideologist and no man of principle, but rather a *bonvivant,* a non-intellectual, and a naturally gifted storyteller.

The years he had spent in France were not creatively fruitless. On the contrary, there he wrote *Nikita's Childhood* (1919), which has been described as "the last work in the autobiographical vein about Russian gentry life" and which many critics have praised as his best work. In France he also embarked upon a more ambitious project, a trilogy of novels, in which he attempted to sum up the experience of Russia during the War, the Revolution, and the Civil War. This work was eventually published under the title of *The Road to Calvary* (1923). But, in this trilogy, Alexey Tolstoy came up against that same problem of "actuality" which he had found so difficult to overcome during the war years. Though the book contains many fine passages and interesting situations as well as background of documentary value, Tolstoy appears happiest in the initial Petersburg stages. The trilogy on the whole lacks depth and is, in the final part, fragmentary.

4

Before we rediscover Alexey Tolstoy in the rapidly changing Soviet environment, we must say something more about his early work and the stories of which this volume is composed.

A Week in Turenevo and Other Stories contains five stories, four of which were written in 1910-13. These early stories, *A Week in Turenevo, Arkhip, The Ravines* and *Mikusha Nalymov,* have a unity of feeling, character and background, all the genuine flavor of the early Alexey Tolstoy and his very special world of traditional lore blended with everyday realism and a sensitive description of nature. Here we have the world of Alexey Tolstoy's childhood—that of the trans-Volga country estate, its oral traditions and anecdotes, its bizarre incidents, eccentric and sometimes lunatic characters, its patient peasants who suffer their masters' wilfulness or violently turn against them with hands, torch or knife. The atmosphere is still distinctly feudal, but it is also rather confused and irrational as though these particular landowners had lost all sense of aim and purpose in life. Not all Russian country gentlemen, or even a quarter of them, could have been quite as fatalistically madcap, crazy or witless, as Mikusha Nalymov charging through his woods with a hunting horn, Sobakin with his simpleton's timidity and trust in *Arkhip,* or Nikolushka Turenev with his utter lack of responsibility; for, otherwise, the whole of the Russian countryside would have been bedlam.

But Alexey Tolstoy was not being satirical or grinding an axe; and there is no immediate social message to be deduced from his pages. What he portrays is the Russian countryside or, rather, that part of it which he saw, felt, and *heard* (for he has an excellent ear for language) at first-hand, at folk-hand, and at literary-hand. No doubt characters like Mikusha Nalymov had existed in real life, but in Alexey Tolstoy's pages he stands out in almost legendary proportions, like some epical Vassily Buslayev who has gone to seed, aimless and undecided, and ventures not as far as the Jordan.

The point could also be made that Alexey Tolstoy was describing a region which had not often, if at all, been described before in Russian literature. As Maxim Gorky has said, the Russian classical writers confined themselves mainly to descriptions of the country estates, landowners and peasants, of the Moscow and Orel provinces, the more "civilized" parts. The Volga region, it must be admitted, was a little wilder and not so "high society;" and the oral tradition and the folk-element which Tolstoy incorporates in his tales has a very feudal flavor. But then it must be borne in mind that the mediaeval element in Russia has survived in places until our day. And Alexey Tolstoy's childhood days were only some twenty years removed from 1861 when serfdom was officially abolished. Many an older man he must have met, landlord or peasant, had had experience and memory of those more tyrannical times. Power, they say, corrupts. Many of Alexey Tolstoy's characters in these stories are weak, capricious men, sometimes tinged with insanity according to modern standards, but they are not monsters: their weakness and final impotence, as in the case of Mikusha Nalymov, make them pitifully or even comically human in the end. If some of the women seem harder and soberer despite their failings, like Anna Mikhailovna in *A Week in Turenevo* or even Olenka in *The Ravines*, that is also true in other Russian novelists.

In 1902, at the age of twenty, Alexey Tolstoy wrote *Once in the Night*, a very short tale not included in this volume. As many writers' early works do, this particular story provides a clue to that world which Tolstoy made his own. It is almost an anecdote and obviously based on local tradition. It must date back to the days of serfdom. "It was the custom for peasant girls, after their wedding ceremony, to be taken to spend their bridal night with the squire, who loved that their pure maidenly bodies should also smell of church incense." This compact sentence contains not only the kernel of the tragedy that is then described, but is also alive with psychological paradoxes, which Alexey Tolstoy here is content to state rather than probe.

Similarly, in *A Week in Turenevo*, we are struck by the paradoxical and tragi-comic relationship between master and peasant, which we find expressed in the conversation held between Anna Mikhailovna and the five peasants who are old "buddies" of her's:

"Well, what's the good news, men?"

"It's like this," said one of them, a bald-headed, puffy-faced peasant, "we have come to you, Anna Mikhailovna," he groaned and looked at his companions.

"If it's about the meadows, men, I have made my last offer. I can't take any less; well, perhaps I can come down three rubles, if you like. . . ."

"No, it's not about the meadows," the first man said again, "we'll stand by what we decided about the meadows, we don't want to swindle you. . . . We've come about this. . . ."

8

He stopped, hesitated and the others also began to hem and haw.

"Whatever are you talking about, I can't understand you?"

"Our fellows are getting out of hand, they're going to set fire to property, Anna Mikhailovna."

"Whose property?"

"Yours, Anna Mikhailovna. That's why we have come to visit Your Honor. Don't be offended—but we're going to burn you up this week."

"That's true," the other peasants chimed in, "it's already been decided: on Friday or Saturday we shall set fire to Anna Mikhailovna's."

Auntie leaned on the writing desk wrapt in thought. The peasants were clearing their throats. One of them stepped forward, lifted up the skirt of his drab, homespun coat and wiped his nose on it.

"Will you burn the barns or the house?" Auntie asked at last.

"The house? God forbid! The barns of course."

An even stranger relationship is to be observed in the story, *Arkhip,* where the landowner Sobakin allows his future murderer to manage his estate until the day of doom. Sobakin, who at the beginning displays some energy in trying to recapture a stolen horse, turns out to be a weakling in human affairs and a nitwit where his estate is concerned. But perhaps unconsciously he wanted to live with death at his elbow?

In the description of Zavalishin's childhood in *The Ravines,* of the early years he spent on an estate in the steppes, of the old spreading manor house and the luxuriating garden, we probably catch some glimpses of Alexey Tolstoy's own boyhood in Sosnovka, we are told of his romantic daydreams, and his sudden and overwhelming enchantment by nature—an enchantment stimulated by his intense reading of Turgenev and then Gogol. Turgenev seems to have exercised the most influence on his young and impressionable mind. But the world of Alexey Tolstoy, as depicted in these stories, is vastly different from Turgenev's. The stability, order and social ease, are gone; there is little cultural or intellectual preoccupation; and there is a thinner dividing line between the landowner and peasant. A Gogol-like aroma of disintegration pervades the scene. It may be the locality which Tolstoy describes or the more general fact that in Tolstoy's day the feudal foundations had become even more sapped and insecure. Whatever the cause, in *A Week in Turenevo,* as well as in *The Ravines,* the manor house is already in a state of decay. The mice are multiplying in the old Turenev mansion where the old drawing-room is now being used to store grain. It is the novel of the manor house which is now inhabited by ghosts.

Yet Alexey Tolstoy's "ghosts" are very robust in their own way. What they lack in brains, they make up in body. They are very physical, full-fleshed, and strangely alive in their own world. One is not quite sure whether their world is real, but they themselves are very real. Many of them live in the past, but their past is vivid. They have very little objective sense and no points of reference to the larger world outside of them: they indulge and splurge without counting the cost; they never deny their emotions and, in the end, love is their only grace and salvation, if they can find it. If they don't, they more often than not meet a violent end. Their thoughtless lives are answered by unexpected death. Yet as they impress themselves physically upon our consciousness, witlessly bent upon their own destruction, they carry with them a swarm of unasked and unanswered questions which we cannot help but meditate.

5

From 1923 to his death in 1945, Alexey Tolstoy lived in the Soviet Union where Moscow had become the new literary capital. To survive in the Soviet Union during these years of change, pressure and constant internal strife, required great flexibility and adaptability. And there was no escaping the impact of "actuality," particularly in the late twenties when Stalin launched his Five Year Plan drives. At first, in the easier atmosphere of *Nep,* Alexey Tolstoy tried his hand at

10

fantasy in books of scientific fiction like *Aelita* which was written round some imaginary inhabitants of Mars. However, this was hardly his right genre, and his intruders from earth remain more convincing than his Martians. In *Ibycus*, he also narrated in a light vein the exploits of a revolutionary profiteer: but this was not really his genre either, though it had an element of his natural exuberance. In these works, as in his *The Manuscript under the Bed, The Murder of Antoine Rivaut* and *Black Friday,* all written between 1922-27, Alexey Tolstoy demonstrated that an experienced and observant writer could deal adequately with themes which did not really correspond with the more subjective structure of his mind. Later, in the 1930's, he also wrote a novel about the defense of Tsarytzin during the civil war, in which inevitably the role played by Stalin was colored in a decisive light.

But none of these works typify his fundamental development. This came with his novels about *Peter the Great,* in which Alexey Tolstoy definitely turns into an historical novelist and, later, in the *Ivan the Terrible* plays, into an historical dramatist as well. In a sense, history provided Tolstoy with an escape from the immediate pressures of the day, but it was not only an escape, for it was also a school of realism and a subject matter that was more related to his original world of eccentrics and manor houses. Peter the Great was a mighty eccentric, too, but one with a fixed aim and a ruthless purpose to pursue.

Alexey Tolstoy did not embark upon his historical novel lightly. As a matter of fact he had touched upon the age of Peter already in some short stories of his, *Peter's Day* and *The Flood,* as far back as 1917. But in the middle 1920's he began doing serious research and concentrated on this subject for almost twenty years. The first volume of *Peter the Great* was published in 1930 and the second in 1934. The third volume was still unfinished on his death. The war years, when Tolstoy was increasingly playing the part of the public man, no doubt interrupted the work on this final volume.

It must not be forgotten, however, that the historical theme was a somewhat dubious project in the 1920's and an ambiguous one in the 1930's. Many marxist critics of the 1920's, under the influence of Pokrovsky's economic view of history, looked unfavorably upon great historical figures, while other critics tended to cavil at most interpretations of those figures. Alexey Tolstoy was not therefore treading an easy path whether of escape or contribution. And that he wrote a play on the same subject made it all the more a controversial one. In fact, his *Peter the Great* was much assailed between 1920 and 1932, especially by the vociferous R.A.P.P. critics. As he says himself, "The staging of the first version of *Peter* in the filial of the Arts Theatre was met hostilely by R.A.P.P., and it was saved by comrade Stalin when, already in 1929, he gave a correct historical interpretation of the age of Peter." * As we know, Stalin was then about to overthrow the marxist historical school of the 1920's and to substitute for it his own version of "concrete history," which admitted the efficacy of great men. At any rate, Alexey's Tolstoy's *Peter* seems to have played into Stalin's hands, though there is no evidence of any collusion. After 1932, and even more after Maxim Gorky's death, Tolstoy became an increasingly prominent figure on the literary and public scene. He became an Academician, a member of the Supreme Soviet, and a chairman of the War Crimes Commission. He enjoyed all the comforts that the Soviet Union could provide, but he never became a "voice of authority" or a "voice of conscience" as Gorky had been. It was a long road from *A Week in Turenevo* to *Peter the Great,* "the first real historical novel of the Soviet age," as Gorky called it. And yet in some ways it was a short road for the former Count and squire, who certainly felt more at home in the old Russia of his own childhood, as well as in mythology and history, than among the Petersburg intellectuals or the Moscow bolsheviks.

[1] Quoted from page 46 of *Soviet Literature Toady* by George Reavey. Yale University Press.

A WEEK IN TURENEVO

Auntie Anna Mikhailovna always kept a plateful of bread-crumbs soaked in milk under her washstand to discourage the mice from eating the soap; and under no circumstances would Auntie allow mousetraps to be brought into the house; about a mouse she would say:

"It's a living creature, after all. If you put it into a trap, the trap may go bang across its belly."

Apart from the washstand Auntie's bedroom was furnished with chiffoniers in the corners—on one of them there was a watch stand with great-grandfather's watch on it—over the bed hung a tapestry depicting two borzoi hounds and on a bedside table there was a small round box full of cigarettes.

Auntie smoked a cheap, strong tobacco which she thought was not injurious to her health. She loved to go out to the porch, light a cigarette, and gaze at the greyish poplars beyond the pond and at the blue smoke curling over the village.

Her bedroom door opened into a broad, low passage where the servants' rooms used to be in the old days; at the end, a spiral staircase led to the nine rooms above, which had once been occupied by the owner's family; nobody ever went there any more and the wooden latticework on the drawing-room walls that had once been covered with plush, the huge, cave-like fireplaces, the tall bookcases in the library, the tables and chairs piled on top of each other in the corner—everything was covered with a thick layer of dust, for, in all these rooms, grain lay a couple of feet thick on the floors and the mice reigned supreme.

Sometimes, in the night, the beams would crack under the weight of the grain and Auntie, in a petticoat, her hair in a bun on top of her head, would go with a candle to see which beam had cracked.

They were used to noises in that house, however. Old, ailing Daryushka, the housekeeper, would only cross herself sleepily in the kitchen, believing that it was Pyotr Petrovich's ghost, the mistress' great-grandfather, clumping about the house—the old man whose portrait showed him on crutches, in a brightly-colored dressing gown, his eyebrows grown together over the bridge of his nose—in general he looked like a bird of prey.

Pyotr Petrovich's was probably not the only ghost that strode about the house on autumn nights, up to its knees in grain; there must have been many ghosts who looked with sorrow on the now deserted manor house at Turenevo which had once been so full of life; but there was nobody left to scare, nobody to complain to. . . .

All were dead and gone, and had taken their pleasures, their riches and their unfulfilled dreams into the cold earth with them; and that lonely old soul, Auntie Anna Mikhailovna, the last of them, lived all alone in the spacious Turenev Manor House. Every evening she used to go out and watch the mist rise from the water meadows beyond the Volga until it enshrouded the garden, the columned summerhouse and the bit of rope hanging from the swing, and then reached the porch.

With her hands thrust into the pockets of a straight, grey jacket, Auntie would walk along the selfsame avenue every night. Her cigarette would go out and stay out. When it would get too dark to see the trees, it was time for bed.

Auntie would go to her bedroom, break up bread for the mice, say her prayers and get into bed; she would not fall asleep immediately, but would lie awake a long time, thinking of the past—the faces of loved ones long since passed away arose before her; or she would think of the sins she had

14

committed that day or of her only nephew, the unfortunate Nikolushka, and wonder what he was doing. Or, as she lay thinking, she racked her brains about how she was to meet her bills. This business of making ends meet had been her chief preoccupation since girlhood.

This evening, before Anna Mikhailovna had time to get into bed, she heard the sound of carriage bells approaching. Auntie listened.

"Who can be coming here so late? It can't be Afrikan Ilyich? But, then, who else could it be?"

Slipping on an old skirt (she had no other, for on Sundays anybody could ask Auntie for anything they wanted, and a whole week before the village women would plan to get one of her better skirts from her), Anna Mikhailovna went down to the kitchen, but to her astonishment found none of the girls who lived in the house without anything special to do; a tall, round-shouldered man in a long, brown traveling coat was already in the doorway. He came in and began shaking off the dust, which is so thick and abundant in the trans-Volga area that, when a traveler arrives, one cannot tell whether it is a Negro or just simply the devil himself.

When he had wiped his face, the man actually did turn out to be Afrikan Ilyich, whose skin was naturally a dark brown. Bending over Auntie's hand, he said in a light tone:

"Here I am, Your Excellency."

Anna Mikhailovna kissed the close-cropped round head of which Afrikan Ilyich was so proud; "Now that's a head, not the sort young men have of today," he used to say. Fearing to show pleasure that was not proper towards a man tired from a journey, Auntie merely said to him:

"It is good that you have come, Afrikan Ilyich, we'll have the samovar ready in a minute. Those girls of mine are a nuisance, they run around at nights."

"Not a bad idea, the samovar," said Afrikan Ilyich in a grating voice; he went into the dining room where he cast a look of satisfaction at the unusual sideboard shaped like a

15

Noah's Ark, at the sleeping flies on the wall and at the glass of warm kvass on the window sill. Everything was the same as it had always been.

Auntie brought in plates of food, opened and closed the doors of the sideboard, fussed around helplessly and breathlessly until Afrikan Ilyich shouted to her:

"Sit down, Your Excellency! You have four silly girls sitting in the kitchen and you are fussing around. . . ."

Auntie immediately sat down with a sweet smile which gave her oval, lined face a look of tenderness.

"I have some news," said Afrikan Ilyich. "I will tell you as soon as I have eaten."

He poured half of his glass of vodka into his cupped palms, rubbed his hands on a napkin until it became as black as soot, swallowed the other half, cleared his throat and bit at a pickled mushroom. Auntie's mushrooms were wonderful.

"What's the news?" asked Auntie. Is it something about Nikolushka?"

Afrikan Ilyich, however, began telling her an interesting story that he had just read in a newspaper, he ate and drank between the words, dragging them out to their full length while Auntie looked into his eyes as she listened patiently, smiling thoughtfully and wondering whom the news was about. When Afrikan Ilyich had finished his story and began describing the Zemstvo Congress at Melekes, how much they had drunk there, Auntie asked cautiously:

"My friend, when are you going to tell me about what you promised?"

Afrikan Ilyich frowned terribly.

"Tomorrow Nikolai and Nastasia are coming. That's the news for you."

"Lord Jesus!" Auntie crossed herself.

"They did not want to come with me in the carriage. They are coming by rail, first class. We must send a carriage to meet them. . . ."

16

"However did they consent?" exclaimed Auntie. "They never wanted to come, no matter how often I wrote."

"Didn't want to?" Afrikan Ilyich snorted and refilled his glass. "Didn't want to? They don't want to die of hunger! Nastasia pawned all her jewels and lost the whole lot at cards in a fortnight, while Nikolushka spent his time in the bar drinking champagne. They have squandered everything to the last thread!"

"How did you manage to persuade them, Afrikan Ilyich?"

"It was quite simple—I bought the railway tickets, Your Excellency. They had about twenty-five rubles left in cash, no more, and they owed money on all sides, at the hotel, at the tailor's and in restaurants. (Auntie began crossing herself frequently.) I told them I would hold the hotel bill and settle it as soon as they were in the railway carriage. They argued that they would be in your way since they were not married, it would not be proper, and so on. I said to Nikolai: you fool, Auntie has written a hundred times to tell you that, if that Nastasia loves you and will give up her former life, then she will be a daughter to Auntie and a wife to you. I was fed up to the teeth with them and went away first. . . . They came yesterday, straight to Krasnov's Hotel. . . . In short, Your Excellency, although everything is as you wished, I consider the whole business nonsense. . . ."

"My friend, it is not nonsense," said Auntie, hurriedly interrupting him. "Nikolushka is honest by nature. (Afrikan Ilyich did not object but scratched the back of his cropped head vigorously.) And Nastasia's heart is not in this noisy life, that's obvious if she agrees to give up Moscow and go with him to some poor old aunt. That's how I understand it. . . . The only thing I'm afraid of is that it will be dull for them here after the capital. . . . Well, I'll do the best I can. . . :"

"Why exert yourself? I suggest that you don't," cried Afrikan Ilyich. "It'll be enough if you feed them. . . ."

Auntie lowered her eyes and blushed.

17

"Don't be angry with me, my friend, let's do the best we can for them," she said softly but finally.

Afrikan Ilyich took Auntie's plump and wrinkled hand, raised it to his bristling lips and kissed it.

"You are a wonderful woman, Your Excellency."

II

As usual Auntie awoke before dawn, lit a candle and began pacing softly up and down the bare boards of her room that had seemed quite strong the day before but were now creaking loudly; she stopped short, afraid that her crazy running to and fro would awaken the whole house.

In order to fill in the time until breakfast she dusted the gold and silver frames of the old icons; since childhood she had been afraid to look at the family icon, a miraculous Redeemer, painted in dark colors with inflexible eyes, in a gem-studded embossed frame. She went through her box of papers with locks of hair belonging to the dear departed. She experienced some painful memories as she hid away a heavy, bone toothpick case. She remembered an old frame amongst her souvenirs, but could not find it.

All these old heirlooms talked in their own pensive language to Auntie Anna Mikhailovna, the youngest and the last of them. Of all her old things the one that Auntie probably loved best of all was the wide, red armchair, upholstered in cloth, with a spring sticking out of it. Auntie and her nine deceased sisters had all been nursed in that chair.

"So the trial has come," thought Anna Mikhailovna, sitting down in the chair. "Shall I have the strength to turn such fly-by-nights on to the path of truth? Nastyenka, she is probably easier to deal with—she lived in sin, fell in love and that purified her soul. She abandoned her rich admirers and sold her property, that means she had fallen in love. But Nikolenka, he's the trump card. Calls for champagne when he hasn't a farthing in his pocket. Just try and teach him to work. I don't want work, he'll say, give me pigeon's milk. I'll have to introduce him to our priest, let them talk together. Father Ivan is a man of great moral strength. I mustn't put it off. As soon as they come I must call Father Ivan."

Auntie was excited and could not sit still, so she went out into the passage where it was cooler.

The lamp hanging from an iron ring in the ceiling was turned down low but was still burning. Through a half-open door she could hear Afrikan Ilyich snoring as loud as though a bumblebee were in his nose. Dark-eyed Mashutka, Auntie's favorite, was sleeping on a trunk, her knees uncovered and one thin arm hanging down.

"She's tossing about so," whispered Auntie, bending over her dusky face and straightening the patchwork quilt that had fallen off her. The girl's eyelashes cast a shadow on her cheek and her childish mouth was half open.

"Such a beauty, the Lord be with you. . . ." Auntie stood meditating. Suddenly her legs gave way from under her in fear. "But no," she thought and shook her head in the dark passage, "I will not let you come to any harm. . . ."

Upstairs the mice were running about in the grain. She wanted her tea. But dawn was only just breaking. Auntie went back to her room and lit a cigarette; she was thinking hard and blinking her eyes frequently.

A hard day had begun. Mashutka, who had been sent up to the roof to keep a lookout, reported that "nobody at all was to be seen except Granddad Fyodor with a piebald cow tied behind his cart."

Afrikan Ilyich came to breakfast, looking tired and angry. He sat sideways on his chair, sipped his tea, sighed and smoked hand-rolled cigarettes.

"Darya!"he called at last.

"Daryushka's down in the cellar, I'll go and give orders myself."

"What orders will you give? You don't even know what orders to give, Your Excellency."

"Horses. . . ." said Auntie softly. "You are tired, my friend,

19

and you are coughing. I think I will go to the station myself. I assure you, it will even be good for me to get out into the fresh air. I sit here all the time, a regular homebird."

Afrikan Ilyich thrust out his jaw and fixed his bearlike eye on the quiet, but not timid Auntie; there is no knowing how the dispute would have ended had not a carriage suddenly arrived at the house.

Everybody hurried out to the porch. Afrikan Ilyich, a cigarette in his mouth and one eye screwed up, stood there with his hands in his pockets; behind his back four bareheaded girls in red blouses stood whispering; Auntie, her narrow shoulders shuddering as though from cold, was smiling kindly, her eyes like two narrow slits.

Nikolushka, wearing a long, camel-haired coat, rested a kid-gloved hand on the driver's box and climbed heavily out of the carriage; walking with his legs wide apart like a cavalryman he hurried to embrace his aunt.

On a high pile of cushions sat Nastya, a thin, beautiful woman, with a small pale face and eyes like grey glass, which always looked surprised. Auntie went to the carriage and held out her hand to the young woman.

"At last God has brought us together. Welcome home!"

Nastya, hastily holding up her dress, jumped down on to the grass.

"We had already given you up," said Auntie, leading the newcomers to the rooms that had been prepared for them and from which Mashutka with her two buckets fled in fright.

Afrikan Ilyich followed behind.

"We've been waiting a long time," he said hoarsely. "We waited at breakfast and at lunch. The lunch was a good one, we ate it all up. . . ."

III

Nikolushka walked up and down the room with his heavy cavalryman's gait, flung his arms about and shrugged his shoulders. His rosy face with its full mouth and ridged eyebrows would have been handsome if it had not been for a slight puffiness of his cheeks and his shifty eyes, which were big and grey. He was very verbose and eloquent.

"My soul is a wilderness, my life is twisted and broken. I am bearing the burden of one whom I love, a creature who is helpless and tired. We were on the brink of ruin, Auntie. You have held out your hand to us. Today, within these ancestral walls, I feel a fresh stream of energy. I believe in the future."

Auntie, greatly excited, sat in her armchair. Behind her stood Afrikan Ilyich, puffing clouds of smoke from his cigarette. . . . Nastyenka was hidden in the shadows behind the bed.

"Auntie, teach me to live, teach me to work and you will save me and this unfortunate woman."

Anna Mikhailovna took Nikolushka by the hand, pulled him down beside her on the chair and for some time did not speak.

"Nikolai," she said at last, "do you know what earth is?"

Nikolushka looked at her in astonishment and bit his lips.

"That's just it, you don't know. In that city of yours you probably never walk on the earth, you walk on stones all the time. Your forefathers, Nikolushka, never went away from the land. It was quite an occasion when they went to Simbirsk, and they never went more than once or twice a year for the elections or to see about a mortgage or a sale. . . . And they were ashamed even to think of boredom or idleness. The earth is your cradle, you came from the earth and to it you must return. . . ."

Nikolushka bowed his head, sighing deeply. He felt uncomfortable sitting in the same chair with Auntie and, besides, Afrikan Ilyich was smoking strong tobacco close to him.

"Don't you worry about our estate being ruined, we'll put all that right. Afrikan Ilyich has that matter in hand and never rests, for which he deserves the thanks of all our Turenev family. And you can begin with the smaller things, that may

21

be of some help. You can catch crayfish and preserve them, send them to the city—that's a profitable business. Or you can plant mushrooms, the expensive kinds. Or breed hares: the meat we can use as food and the skins can be sent abroad where, they say, Russian hares fetch a good price, they make ermine out of them; it's true what I say, isn't it, Afrikan Ilyich?"

"Absolutely true, Your Excellency."

"There's plenty you can find to do if you only have the will. And in about twenty years our woods will have grown and we'll be on our feet again. Get down to work, get down to it, my friend—you'll save the estate and make a man of yourself. There was Solovyov, a philosopher, he was just like you in his youth, did not believe in God, but he worked and gained belief. . . . ."

At this point Auntie, greatly excited, rose from her chair.

"You will believe in God. It is the fashion nowadays not to believe in God. But I say—there is a God!"

As she said these words Anna Mikhailovna brought her hand down hard on the chest of drawers. Afrikan Ilyich hid himself in a cloud of smoke.

For a time nobody spoke. Then, without warning, the door opened and in walked Father Ivan—tall, thin as a pole, dressed in a dirty sailcloth surplice; he looked over the newcomers without haste and his huge mouth twisted in a grin, revealing yellow teeth, like those of an old horse, under his thin mustache. His face also had something horsey about it, with a heavy jaw and a long upper lip. The only handsome thing about him was his dark eyes, but he deliberately gave them a satirical expression which was the result of confusion rather than derision.

"But," Father Ivan said, "it's fuggy!" As he said these words, his niece Raisa, dressed in a little pink dress, her head a mass of little, blond curls, came gliding into the room for all the world like a pink butterfly.

22

"That's a girl for you!" Afrikan Ilyich said, coughing heavily.

The guests shook hands—Father Ivan offering the whole of his leg-of-mutton fist and Raisa the tips of her fingers. They sat down.

"You see, Father," began Auntie, "the fledgelings have come flying back to the nest. Nikolushka and his wife have come to us for the whole winter."

"I approve," said Father Ivan, "but permit me to ask what reasons prompted you to take such an unusual step?"

"Isn't he spiteful!" chuckled Afrikan Ilyich.

Nikolushka modestly lowered his eyes and answered that he had come to learn to work.

"Useful," Father Ivan said, screwing up his eyes and displaying his horse-teeth.

"In fulfillment of Anna Mikhailovna's desires, I shall make an attempt to elevate myself once more. See," Nikolushka held out his hands, "I can follow the plough. But eternal night still fills my soul. I know life too well to be able to enjoy anything again."

On hearing these words Raisa opened her little mouth and gazed at Nikolushka like a hypnotized bird. A silence fell. Then suddenly, in the shadow behind the bed, Nastya laughed out loud. Father Ivan turned his horse-head towards her in surprise, the cigarette trembled on Auntie's lips.

"There's nothing for you to laugh at," exclaimed Nikolushka angrily. "It's idiotic!"

Father Ivan cleared his throat and began:

"In the course of our conversations, dear Anna Mikhailovna has often expressed the opinion that man, by labour, naturally comes to an understanding of divine providence. I agree but only partly. Last week I was passing along the main road near the place where day labourers were breaking stones. I heard how they were blaspheming and cursing not only the contractor but also the Lord God. Therefore, al-

23

though I must agree with Anna Mikhailovna on the usefulness of labour, I must add—not any kind of labour."

"What a philosopher!" Afrikan Ilyich exclaimed, rolling a cigarette and coughing so hard that he turned a dark red.

"Anna Mikhailovna," came Mashutka's thin voice from outside the door, "supper is served."

IV

After supper Nikolushka went out into the garden, which lay dense and damp under the bright moon that lent a melancholy note to the doleful voices of the tree toads. A female, lovelorn, broke into their chorus abruptly and impertinently. The mist settled on the glade that led down to the river and came creeping through the thick grass.

Nikolushka went into a tumbledown summerhouse overlooking a backwater that was filled by the waters of the Volga every spring and, striking a match, scared the doves nesting under the roof.

From here he could see the water meadows with clumps of mist over the marshes, the black mass of willows by the millpond and, far away, high up on the horizon, the long ribbon on the Volga gleaming in places as though covered with fish scales.

Nikolushka breathed in the tang of the grass, the earth and the marsh flowers, and recalled the distant past. What had happened and what he had probably seen in his dreams as a child merged in sad and lucid recollections.

He remembered how his mother had sat in this summerhouse; he recalled her dark dress that smelt of some old, warm perfume, which no longer existed. This memory was so strong that Nikolushka imagined this forgotten perfume wafted to him through the marshy smell of the buttercups. His mother had put her arms round his shoulders as they watched the moon play on the silver scales of the distant river. Nikolushka had asked in a whisper: "Mama, is it true what the boys told me, that there is a teeny-weeny little old man living in our garden who sells trained frogs at a kopek each?"

"I don't know, perhaps there is an old man like that here," Mamma answered, and a hot teadrop fell on Nikolushka's cheek.

"Are you crying, Mamma?"

"I don't know. I think I am."

At that moment Nikolushka had seen something on a beam under the roof that was either a bird or a little old man who bent his bird's head down and looked at him.

Nikolushka sighed and leaning on the balustrade continued gazing at the hazy outlines of the trees and the sparkling ribbon in the distance. Again he remembered. . . . They were already in town and he was sitting with his feet drawn up on a sofa before the fireplace, watching the yellowish-red flames dance with a slight crackle. Suddenly he heard the doorbell ring and a lady, her wide silk dress rustling as she walked, crossed the drawing room that was lit only by the fire in the grate. At the door of the study stood his father, a tall thin man with an aquiline nose and deep-sunk eyes.

"How kind of you," he said to the lady in a strange voice that annoyed Nikolushka; "how kind of you." He and the lady disappeared behind the door. Nikolushka's heart beat fast in sweet alarm, he felt drawn towards the door. He heard his father's footsteps, his dull abrupt words and the hurried whispering of the lady. . . . Something fell on the floor. A silence followed, then a soulful sigh and the sound of a kiss.

Nikolushka clutched at his throat: he wanted to scream, to run away, to hide his head. . . . In the other door, however, his mother was beckoning to him, she was dressed all in black, like a nun, and stood there abandoned, pale, terrible. He was suddenly so sorry for her—he rushed to her and hugged her knees. . . .

"Go away, go away from here, you mustn't listen," his mother said, and took Nikolushka away to the bedroom.

In the bedroom there was a whole wall covered with icons lit up by several wax candles, and, before them, a low stool with a high back on which to rest the forehead—here his

25

mother would spend hours on her knees. If you touched her dress stealthily with a finger you could feel iron chains under it.

"Never, do you hear me, never must you eavesdrop," his mother whispered impetuously, "your father is a passionate, big-hearted man, it is not for you to judge him."

She made Nikolushka kneel beside her, and he watched the long, fat, yellow flames of the candles. The room smelt of wax and medicines, it was warm, dreamy and boring. . . .

In this way Nikolushka grew up between the icons and the study, where he would run secretly to gaze fearfully, but eagerly at the portrait of a beautiful lady in a mahogany frame, to touch the strange knickknacks on the writing desk and to smell the sharp, astounding odour of a cigar butt.

One day Nikolushka picked up a lady's glove from the carpet and in a fit of incomprehensible excitement kissed it and hid it under his jacket.

Very,very often, in dreams he would see a narrow, empty street bathed in pale light and in the distance the figure of a beautiful woman. . . . He would run after her, leap into the air, and, with swiftly moving legs, fly over the sidewalk. His heart would beat fast, it would miss a beat but the figure would slip farther and farther away and there was no over-taking it.

Nikolushka sighed loudly. A dove, brushing against the branches, flew from under the roof. Somewhere close at hand he could hear the voices of Auntie, Nastya and Raisa.

V

I was absolutely stunned by the way he spoke," Nikolushka heard Raisa's thin voice saying. "Ah, Anna Mikhailovna, you know I haven't seen much, but I found it so interesting . . . so interesting. . . . Especially when he said: 'I have tried every-thing in life, but eternal night still fills my soul. . . .' something seemed to snap in my heart."

Nikolushka watched the women walk up to a bench. Auntie

and Nastya sat down while slender Raisa remained standing, looking at the distant light in the window.

"Lately my heart has been in a flutter all the time," she continued, "and, to tell the truth, Uncle Vanya has grown awfully grumpy. At night he reads, walks about, makes a lot of noise. . . . Or else he begins to talk very loudly—I listen and listen and then the tears come. Ours is a miserable life."

Auntie laughed, drew Raisa towards her, kissed her and sat the girl down alongside her

"You're all so good, Anna Mikhailovna. . . . But I was more sorry for Nikolai Mikhailovich today than for anybody else. . . ."

"Mind you don't fall in love," said Nastya with a snigger.

Auntie immediately began in her businesslike manner.

"Come on to bed, Nastyenka, you are sneezing already. And you too, Raisa, off you go to bed."

"Anna Mikhailovna, I would like to sit here a little longer, it is very nice here. Uncle Vanya will call me when it is time to go home. May I?"

Auntie laughed again, kissed her and went away with Nastya.

With weary steps Nikolushka came out of the summer-house. Raisa saw him, gasped, started to rise from the bench but sat down again.

"Are you admiring the night?" said Nikolushka sitting down beside the girl and resting his chin on his walking stick. "God grant that you may never know sorrow. How I envy your youth. How many beautiful dreams you still have ahead of you! You long for a beautiful life and are afraid—can it be that it too will collapse and fall into a mire?" He stole a glance at Raisa. She was sitting and nibbling a birch leaf, her eyes lowered. . . .

"Tell me about your life," whispered Raisa in a scarcely audible voice.

"Tell you about my life? . . . All the filth I have been through, all the vices with which I wasted away my youth?

27

No, you must not hear such things. What I need now is the sympathy of a chaste and pure woman to save, perhaps, to preserve the remnants of my living soul."

"Good Lord, what are you saying?"

"Look at this moonlight—that beauty is not for me. I am twenty-eight years old, but my life is over."

He lowered his head. From the house came Nastya's voice: "Nikolai, come to bed. . . ."

Nikolushka raised his head and smiled bitterly.

"There it is, the millstone round my neck. What have I in store—naturally, a downward rush head first to the bottom. Farewell."

He took Raisa's tiny, cold hand, sqeezed it, shook his head hopelessly and walked towards the house along a path that lay patchy in the moonlight.

Just then Raisa was also called in. Father Ivan led her through the old churchyard and across the field, making a beeline for home; he walked with his arms swinging, his head bowed, snorting disgustedly.

"What were you talking about to that, what's his name? . . ." he asked.

"Nikolai Mikhailovich is so unfortunate."

"Aha, and you wept, I suppose?"

"Nothing of the sort. You ought to be ashamed of yourself, Uncle Vanya, to laugh at him. You teach us to love people and yet you speak ill of them yourself."

"What ill did I speak? I did not say a word about him."

"Words are not needed."

"You don't understand anything," said Father Ivan, opening the gate of a garden overgrown with gillyflowers. "You don't understand anything. . . ." He stopped short and gazed towards the smoking meadows beyond the huge sleeping poplars, the crescent of the moon reflected in the water, and the fleecy night clouds that were racing across the sky before dawn like a flock of sheep. "There is nothing, Raisa, that you understand."

28

Auntie Anna Mikhailovna, screwing up her eyes in the tobacco smoke, stood in the room that had been made ready for the young people before two huge leather trunks, the last remnants of Nikolushka's better days, and thought how good it would be to burn it all.

"With what money was it bought? Rags, paint and powder, nothing but dirt, you will start a new life here. . . ."

"So you have found the tramp," she said to Nastya who came in from the garden with Nikolushka. "And the nights, such wonderful nights we have here. Especially in flood time, you just can't leave the balcony until dawn."

Auntie bid them good night, kissed them both, made the sign of the cross over them and was about to leave the room when she suddenly asked:

"What is there in those trunks?"

"In this there are evening and party dresses and in the other shoes, hats and Nikolushka's things."

"And what do you want with all that now?" asked Auntie. "Will you get dressed up here? You should burn all those things, now shouldn't you, eh? We can alter your grandfather's frock coat for you, Nikolushka, and for you, Nastyenka, we can remake a few silk dresses, we can find some old ones here—in fact we can find a lot of things. Oh, well, all right, go to bed, we'll talk about it another time. . . ."

Auntie left the room smiling guiltily. Nastyenka locked the door behind her and with her hands on her hips, a favorite attitude, walked up to Nikolai.

"What do you mean by it," she began, "trying to turn that girl's head? D'you think I don't know how you wept on her shoulder? I know all your foul tricks," she poked him in the forehead with her finger, "that, my dear, is something I will not allow in a decent house."

"Don't you dare poke me in the forehead," said Nikolushka gloomily.

"If you like, I'll scratch that ugly mug of yours for you . . ."

Nikolushka retreated behind the bed and, seeing Nastyenka

advancing towards him, suddenly shouted out in a loud voice:
"Listen, if you don't stop it at once, I'll call Auntie."

VI

Auntie was seated on a high stool before a writing desk
going over the accounts in thick books that had been started
some fifteen years before by her late brother Aggei.

Brother Aggei had been uncommonly lazy and usually
spent whole days here beside the writing desk lying on the
sofa; he either did nothing at all or read Alexander Dumas'
Vicomte de Bragelonne and, when he got to the end, he
seemed to have forgotten the beginning and started reading
the book over again. If anybody, who had come on business,
should happen to tap at the little window cut into the office
wall while he was thus engaged, Aggei would turn over
heavily so that the sofa springs creaked and would say:

"What do you want, anyway? Why don't you go to the
steward, you can see I'm busy? . . ."

Today, contrary to her usual practice, Auntie was not pay-
ing much attention to her computations and made mistakes.

"A hundred and twenty-three rubles, sixteen kopeks," holding the pen between her teeth she checked the figures off on
an abacus, "sixteen kopeks. Oh, good God, what will it all
come to?"

At this moment five peasants, clumping with their heavy
boots and removing their hats, came into the office; they were
old friends of Auntie's. She put down her pen and greeted
them affably.

"Well, what's the good news, men?"

"It's like this," said one of them, a bald-headed, puffy-faced
peasant, "we have come to you, Anna Mikhailovna," he
groaned and looked at his companions.

"If it's about the meadows, men, I have made my last offer.
I can't take any less; well, perhaps I can come down three
rubles, if you like. . . ."

"No, it's not about the meadows," the first man said again,

"we'll stand by what we decided about the meadows, we don't want to swindle you. . . . We've come about this. . . :"

He stopped, hesitated and the others also began to hem and haw.

"Whatever are you talking about, I can't understand you?"

"Our fellows are getting out of hand, they're going to set fire to property, Anna Mikhailovna."

"Whose property?"

"Yours, Anna Mikhailovna. That's why we have come to visit, Your Honour. Don't be offended—but we're going to burn you up this week."

"That's true," the other peasants chimed in, "it's already been decided: on Friday or Saturday we shall set fire to Anna Mikhailovna's."

Auntie leaned on the writing desk engrossed in thought. The peasants were clearing their throats. One of them stepped forward, lifted up the skirt of his drab, homespun coat and wiped his nose on it.

"Will you burn the barns or the house?" Auntie asked at last.

"The house? God forbid, the barns of course."

The oldest of the peasants, Granddad Spiridon, leaning on his long staff, stared at Auntie with eyes watery from inflamed eyelids. His hair was quite white and his thin neck was bound round a dozen times with a woolen scarf.

"I used to go hunting with your daddy, Mikhail Petrovich," he began in a cracked, thin voice, "your daddy killed a wolf. Sometimes he would say: 'Spiridon, get me a horse, the fastest you can find'. . . . He would leap into the saddle and away. . . . Yes I remember it all," he smacked his purple lips, "and your granddad, Pyotr Mikhailovich. . . . I remember them all. . . .

"Come and have some tea with me some time, Spiridon," Auntie said kindly, "we haven't had a heart-to-heart talk for a long time. . . ."

"I'll come, I'll come, Anna Mikhailovna. . . . Now, Mikhail Mikhailovich, your great-granddad, I don't remember him. . . ."

"Why do you want to cause me this unpleasantness, men?" Auntie sighed and ran her pencil along the middle of the book, "What wrong have I done you?"

"D'you think we'd have thought of it ourselves," said the peasants; "last week some papers came to the village and the fellows read them—and now they are all wrought up. In them it said that we ought to burn up the masters."

After this they talked about the meadows, about hay-making, about the ploughing for next year until the peasants said good-bye and went away leaving a strong smell of sheepskins and home-grown tobacco behind them. Auntie continued sitting at her desk lost in gloomy thought. When Afrikan Ilyich came in, looking tired and with his waistcoat unbuttoned, she told him quietly what the peasants had been to see her about.

"Let them burn down the barns, they're insured," answered Afrikan Ilyich, yawning broadly.

"The barns don't worry me, my friend, but the attitude."

"The peasants have been led to this by your goodness, Your Excellency. I will go to the District Police Officer immediately."

"Don't go, please, Afrikan Ilyich."

"Excuse me, but I will go."

"I ask you, please don't go."

Then Afrikan Ilyich planted his feet firmly apart and began to shout at Her Excellency. Nevertheless he did not go. Auntie had the last word: "You can't ruin a living being for the sake of rotten straw," she said and asked him to call Mashutka to the office.

Mashutka came running in and stood beside Auntie, placing her suntanned hand on the writing desk.

"Did you call me, Auntie?"

"Listen," Anna Mikhailovna said, patting her hand, "you understand that God always knows who tells the truth and who lies, and He punishes those who tell untruths."

32

"I'll always remember it," answered Mashutka merrily.

"So you do know—and how do you behave?"

"When had I lied, Auntie?"

"Of course you haven't told a lie. But listen. . . . What did you talk to the young master about this morning? Eh?"

Mashutka lowered her eyes and scratched the writing desk with her fingernail.

"Nikolai Mikhailovich asked me how old I was. . ."

"And what did you tell him?"

"Sixteen. . . ."

"And what else?"

"He asked me if I had a silk shawl. . . ."

"And what did you say to that?"

"I told him I hadn't."

"Well, listen," said Auntie sternly, "the young master likes joking with you. . . . Don't you bother him, don't cross his path too often. Understand?"

Anna Mikhailovna closed the books, told Mashutka to go and sat for a long time shaking her head and looking through the window at the sparrows fluttering and twittering in the lilacs outside. "I'm going to have a hard job with them all," she thought.

As Anna Mikhailovna was leaving the office she collided with Nikolushka in the doorway:

"Auntie, for God's sake give me some work to do. . . ." he said in the voice of a convalescent.

"What work can I give you, young man? Rest a bit first and eat your fill. . . ."

"I see you have a library upstairs. . . . I could start by putting that in order."

"You'll be doing me a favour, my friend, and I thank you in advance. Your grandfather always wanted to sort out the books. . . . I'll send people to help you right away," and Auntie went away in high spirits to make arrangements about the help.

VII

There was grain on the library floor a couple of feet thick; thick dust covered the bookcases, the windows and the cornices; trails made by mice led in all directions on the table tops.

Matvei, the coachman, and the girls shovelled the grain out of the library into the drawing room. They raised thick clouds of dust that turned their faces grey; the startled mice scuttled over the sweet-smelling grain; little pink baby mice trembled in the nests that were laid open; a frightened dove circled under the ceiling, brushing its wings against the broken chandelier.

"That will do," Nikolushka said, wiping his perspiring face, "sweep up now and go."

They opened the library windows and the evening air, smelling of the fields, flooded the musty room. Standing on a stepladder, Nikolushka opened the narrow glass doors of the first bookcase—the remnants of mouse-eaten books floated lightly to the floor.

"Oh!" shouted Mashutka, brushing the paper fragments from her clothes.

Nikolushka turned round and saw the girl standing under the stepladder looking covertly at the young master.

"What are you doing here?" asked Nikolushka and seizing the chewed-up paper threw it at Mashutka. "Did you see that?"

"We've only just swept up, sir, and you're making a mess again," said Mashutka tossing back her plait.

"Let me brush you down."

He moved down a couple of steps, bent over, ruffled Mashutka's hair and chucked her lightly under her round chin.

"I'll tell the mistress," Mashutka said in a whisper but did not move away.

Nikolushka laughed and, opening a second bookcase where the mice had not been, with some difficulty pulled out a book bound in yellow, gold-embossed leather.

34

"What are you going to do with the books?" Mashutka asked.

"I'm going to read them, silly, here, listen: *The Seven Secrets of Nature* by Eckharthausen. And there is the *Travels of Anacharsis the Younger*. Understand? And here," Nikolushka came down the ladder and sat on the bottom step, *"Neonila or the Profligate Daughter."*

"What's that?"

"Listen. . . . 'Having ruined the noble cavalier Vicomte de Zarnaut with her cruel profligacy, she vainly continued intrigues as disgusting to men as to the Creator, who made this despicable creature'. . . ."

Mashutka looked at a picture of Neonila lying face-down in bed without her shift and, beside her, a chambermaid preparing the apparatus for relieving the stomach while in the door stood the Chevalier de Zarnaut; she moved nearer and breathed on Nikolushka's cheek. . . .

" '. . . but the wanton was possessed of such perfect beauty,' " continued Nikolushka, " "that no mortal could resist her allurements. . . .' "

Mashutka was breathing so close to him and her plait of hair touched Nikolushka's cheek so gently that, looking into her innocent eyes, he pulled her towards him and kissed her on her half-open, cool lips.

It so happened that Auntie, wishing to let some fresh air into the dusty drawing room, opened the balcony door and, as she came in, saw Mashutka leaning back with her hands on Nikolushka's shoulders and he intoxicated with the kiss; the books lay scattered on the floor around them. Auntie screamed. . . . Mashutka gasped and fled. Nikolushka began to rub his nose energetically.

"Nikolai!" Auntie exclaimed walking excitedly up and down the library. "I took Masha into my house to work and am entirely responsible for her, she's sixteen years old, understand? . . . I know you are young and your blood boils.

Mashutka is beautiful. . . . But what do you want? Isn't one woman enough for you? How did you manage to fix yourself up like this? Swear on the cross, this very minute," and Auntie pulled a bunch of little icons and crosses out of her blouse, "swear on the cross that you will never touch Mashutka again! I will not let you go until you give me your word of honour!"

Nikolushka was thoroughly scared and swore: Auntie turned away to the window where the cross of the Turenevo Church, old and modest, glowed in the sunset through the green of the birch trees. Nastya and Raisa were walking together in the garden.

Nastya had wrapped the corner of her Angora shawl round Raisa's shoulders and was bending low over the girl, talking to her.

"Don't believe a single word he says, my dear. . . . He is a marvel at weaving wonder out of words: he pretends to be so unfortunate that you listen to him, you listen and bawl like a fool. . . . I know his character inside out, I see through him as though he were made of glass . . . he can't get on without talking, that's his nature. In fact that's what we came here 'for, to talk. . . ."

"No, I tell you he is unhappy," said Raisa.

"He's unhappy? . . . Now, my dear, you're still only a child. . . . How is he unhappy when the women flock round him like they do." Nastya snorted. "When I got hold of him, an old woman was in love with him, you understand, and he took everything she had and drove her away, my dear, drove her out of the house. . . ."

Raisa turned her face away and walked on for a while without speaking. Nastya kept stealing glances at her and then swiftly unbuttoned the sleeve of her blouse and turned it back to the elbow.

"Here's something for you to admire, just look how he treats me. . . . See this horrible scar, along my whole arm. . . ." Almost in tears she pressed her lips to the pink line on her arm, sucked it and angrily turned down her sleeve.

36

"I will never forgive him for that scar, as long as I live. . . .
When he gets mad, he doesn't know whether he's handling a
dog or a human being. . . . The prison cell has been crying
for him for a long time. . . . One day I shall take him to
court. . . ."

"Good Lord," Raisa cried out, "what are you telling me!"

"And what do you care? Are you sorry for him?"

"I don't know. . . . You're not telling me the truth. . . .
I know you're just talking that way. . . ."

"So you've fallen in love with him, have you? . . . So that's
it. You ought to have told me that at first. We'll start on a
different sort of talk, then. . . ."

Nastya had already let go of Raisa's shoulder and she
placed her hands on her hips and frowned; she was not
destined to continue the conversation. Raisa sat down quickly
on a bench, bent over with her elbows on her knees and her
face in her hands, her shoulders trembling from sobs. . . .

Nastya looked at her and wrinkled her nose: Raisa's shoulders were narrow and, in general, she looked like a little
chicken. . . . Nastya lit a cigarette, drew at it deeply a few
times and then hurled it into the grass; she sat down impetuously beside the girl and took her by the shoulders.

"Listen. . . . Don't you bawl because of that devil. . . . I
shan't give him to you anyway, you know that yourself. . . .
And if I did, you'd only weep your eyes out on account of
him. Stop it, then. . . ."

VIII

Nikolushka was sent to the woods for an airing. When he
had learnt that the peasants were going to burn Auntie up,
he screamed and raved and armed himself with a shotgun to
the terror of all the girls in the kitchen; it had cost Auntie a
great deal of trouble to persuade him to give up his idea of
dealing with the peasants. She took the gun away from him
and said:

"What you ought to do, my friend, is take a look at our

37

property. Look at the woods: Afrikan Ilyich assures me that in fifty years that forest will be a gold mine."

The cart, which was brought to the porch for Nikolushka, rattled as though it were loaded with old iron. Auntie accompanied him to the gates.

"Go along, go along, young man, get a breath of fresh air. . . ."

The village gate was closed. Nikolushka shouted for a long while for someone to open it. At last a bowed ancient came out of a straw shelter, took out his hat and looked at the traveler.

"Hi, Granddad, open the gate!" Nikolushka shouted angrily.

"All right, I'm coming in a minute!" The old man unhurriedly removed a bast loop and opened a gate that squeaked on a dozen different notes. "Where are you from, sir? . . ."

Nikolushka did not answer, but hit the horse with the reins and drove rapidly downhill; the old man gazed after him for a long time—his sight was bad and, as for hearing, he hadn't heard anything for years. . . .

The woods of which Afrikan Ilyich had spoken had really once been a magnificent pine forest—but that was in old Turenev's time. In the autumn trees for masts were selected and bound round at the base with wire so they would swell with resin and become as hard as iron and amber-colored, and in January they were felled. Nikolushka, pulling the reins constantly from under the tail of his lazy nag that kept shaking its head back and forth to keep off the horseflies, saw nothing but a sorry growth of young pine and a consumptive-looking hazel grove along a gully where peasant horses were nipping the trees; when they saw the cart, they jumped farther away from the road on their hobbled feet.

"Hi, young fellow, where is the Turenev Woods here?" Nikolushka asked a herdsman's boy who sat on a tree stump.

"What?"

"The woods, I said, where are the woods, idiot? . . . Our woods?"

"That there's the woods," the boy replied, pushing his cap forward on to his nose.

Nikolushka shrugged his shoulders and drove on until the forest became denser; there he wound the reins round the cart rail, alighted with difficulty and walked over the soft crackling pine needles that carpeted the forest. All round him were stumps, trees with crooked trunks and young saplings; the wind moaned sadly overhead, clouds floated across the blue sky. Sadly Nikolushka crossed a gully overgrown with ferns and lay down on the high ground, his hands under the back of his head. . . .

Alas, gone for ever were the good times—the sleepless nights, the lights on the broad avenues, the snow, the odour of perfumes and furs, the pleasure of fine linen and the slippery silk of evening frocks. . . . The glass doors of the restaurant thrown wide open by the usually scared-looking porter, the hall of the restaurant where the music strained all one's nerves and played on them drunkenly. . . . The lights of the chandeliers, the glittering diamonds, the warm beauty of women's shoulders. . . . The sweating bucket and the gold-necked bottle covered with a snow-white napkin. . . . The intoxicating hum of voices. . . . And in the smoky gloom of a mirror scratched all over by diamonds, red tunics, flying fiddle bows, flowers, and women's eyes dark as a soul stirred by music, black coffee and mad desire. . . .

Nikolushka screwed up his eyes, shook his head and sat up on the grass; all around him—tree stumps, anaemic firs and the pine needles rustling overhead. . . . Dreary indeed was Turenev Woods. . . . Oh, Lord, Oh Lord, what a place to while the time away!

Nikolushka turned over on to his stomach and began to chew a blade of grass. Solitude was rotten, especially in the forest on a hot afternoon. . . . Memories of the past filled

Nikolushka's head—he remembered moments that made the blood seethe in his veins. . . . Only to experience one of those moments and then plunge head down forever in the abyss—in the pupils of mad eyes, in the rustle of silk skirts, in the darkness of feminine fragrance. . . . A cone fell from a tree into the grass right in front of Nikolushka's face. . . . He bit through the blade of grass and laughed bitterly: "Auntie Anna Mikhailovna in her fustian blouse, with her mice and her religious questions. . . . Afrikan Ilyich whose snores fill the house every day after lunch. . . . Rooms piled with grain, books eaten away by mice. . . . Nastyenka whom he knew down to the tiniest birthmark. . . . Brrr. . . . There's not a man could pull himself together under such circumstances. . . . A morass. . . .

A dry branch cracked behind a nearby fir tree. Nikolushka turned quickly round and through the branches saw Raisa's pink frock. . . . The edge of the gingham skirt seemed to sweep him out of his hopeless gloom. . . . Nikolushka jumped up, straightened his jacket and went to Raisa—she had her back to him and was bending down fumbling in the moss. He called her name softly. She straightened up, looked round, gasped and dropped a mushroom from her hand.

"I've come to inspect our wilderness," Nikolushka said, "what are you doing here? . . ."

"I'm gathering mushrooms," Raisa answered, breathing heavily as though from fright, "see, I have got a lot of them, all white, pine mushrooms. . . ."

"They're nice mushrooms. . . . So you like mushrooms?"

"Of course. . . ."

"I'm a city man. . . . I don't know what to look for, I would pick toadstools. . . ."

Raisa blushed a deep red and smiled, throwing her head back slightly and showing her even teeth. . . . Nikolushka could scarcely take his eyes off her tender throat.

"Let us go together," he said, "I'll try and help you."

40

"Oh, no, Nikolai Mikhailovich, that's not a suitable occupation for you. . . ."

"Why is it suitable for you not for me?"

"You're a . . . er . . . city-dweller," said Raisa; she tossed a plait of hair from her chest to her back and walked on.

Nikolushka walked beside her, frowning, his lips pressed bitterly together. . . .

"Now, Raisa, you have reminded me of the most painful thing," he said after a short silence. "But let us not speak about me. . . . It makes no difference, there's no other way for me," as he walked along he broke off a dry twig, snapped it in two and threw it away, "my life is over. . . ."

Raisa bent down, picked a mushroom and thrust it into the basket under a couple of maple leaves.

"People have done me too much harm, have trampled on everything sacred in my soul. . . . Well, I'll have to live here, forgotten, of no use to anybody. . . . And I have not got long to live with my liver. . . . Never mind. . . . And yet sometimes it seems a pity to me that I am not a peasant, healthy, carefree, with an axe in my hands—I'd fell a huge pine and make the chips fly. . . ."

"Stop it, Nikolai Mikhailovich," Raisa whispered in a scarcely audible voice; he could see that her eyes were closed and her lashes wet.

"Raisa, Raya, my darling," he cried in a fervent voice that even astonished him, "you are sorry for me . . . sweetheart. . . ." He seized her little, cold, trembling hands. "Yes? Yes? . . . Oh, help me. . . ."

"How can I help you, I am so foolish, Nikolai Mikhailovich."

"Love me."

These words burst from Nikolushka in an uncontrollable surge, of their own accord. Raisa was in such confusion that she dropped the basket of mushrooms, opened her little mouth, and the tears in her blue eyes immediately dried up. . . .

"Love me," Nikolushka repeated and, dropping to his knees, put his arms around Raisa and lifted his troubled face to her. "You can save me. . . . You will save me. . . . The very first moment you came into the room—pure, innocent, all pink, I realized— I would go out of my mind. . . . Either you or—death. . . ."

Two hours later, Nikolushka ran along the dark passage opening doors and shouting into the empty rooms.

"Aunt. . . . Aunt. . . . Aunt Mikhailovna, where are you?"

"What's bitten you, young man," Auntie asked at last, poking her head out of the box room in the corner.

"I absolutely must talk with you! . . ."

"The Lord help us. . . . You don't look yourself at all!" a dark place that smelt of furs, mothballs and mice, and, without removing his hat, sat down on a trunk; he turned eyes filled with hatred on Nastya who was standing by the window, beside the armchair where she had been talking to Auntie.

"Go away, Nastya," Nikolushka began and suddenly stamped his foot madly on the floor, "go away, I tell you. . . ."

"Have you gone crazy, young man?" asked Nastya, following his glance attentively. Nikolushka jumped up but sat down again. Anna Mikhailovna turned her head first to Nikolushka and then to Nastyenka in bewilderment.

"If that woman does not go away, I shall not be responsible for my actions," he said, swallowing his saliva. Nastya pursed her lips, hid her hands under her kerchief, and walked out.

"Anna Mikhailovna," said Nikolushka, clutching his head between his hands, "Auntie, do you want me to become a man? Do you want me to be young and healthy and earn my living honestly? As long as I have that woman near me I am a corpse. . . . She is drawing me down into the abyss. . . . She, she is the cause of my disgrace. . . ."

"Wait a minute, Nikolai," his aunt interrupted him in a voice that quivered with fright, "speak reasonably . . . my head is in a whirl. . . . What has happened?"

"Auntie, I am going to marry Raisa. . . ."

IX

Auntie's bedroom smelt of valerian drops. Anna Mikhailovna was sitting in an armchair nodding sleepily, a cold bandage round her head. Afrikan Ilyich stood beside her sighing and smoking. Occasionally Auntie sighed, too.

It was after lunch, the hour when the hens and dogs were dozing on the farms and estates, when the people were taking forty winks in the shadow of a fence, in a shed or a carriage house, when some small boy, his shirt tied in a knot at his back, is yawning peacefully on an ash heap, holding a tousled sparrow in his dirty fist; somewhere in a cottage a young woman, big with child, was singing monotonously—before her was a bowl of warm kvass, flies crawling over the table, a sickly smell of onions in the cottage and, through the fly-speckled windows, a view of the same barn and the yellow common. The young woman was sad at heart as she softly dragged out the words of her song; under the window a pig lay listening to her and driving away the tormenting flies with its ragged ear. And now it was Vasilisa the cook singing a similar song on the back porch. Afrikan Ilyich listened in silence until at last he said with a loud sigh:

"How that woman howls, curse her. . . ."

Auntie nodded without opening her eyes.

Yesterday's scene had been hard on her: Nastya had been listening at the door when Nikolushka made his announcement and had burst into the box room like a wild beast. Nikolushka had lost his presence of mind at the sight of those flashing eyes and had turned to Auntie and exclaimed with a sob: "There, you see!"

Then Nastya had struck him in the face with her fist and had got her hands into his hair. Nikolushka spat on her and waved his arms while Auntie self-sacrificingly intervened between the fighting couple and came in for her share: Afrikan Ilyich had come running in, dragged Nastya off Nikolushka and carried her away, she shouting the while: "I'll part your strumpet's hair for her." Nikolushka, first crying on Auntie's shoulder and then on Afrikan Ilyich's waistcoat, again told the whole story of his ruined life. He was given vodka to bring him to his senses. Until long after midnight the old house resounded to sobbing, occasional savage screams, and Auntie's monotonous scolding voice. That same evening Mashutka, despite her fear of ghosts, ran to peep in at the priest's window and afterwards told the girls in the kitchen how, Father Ivan, without his surplice, and wearing only his underpants, had walked up and down the room like a heron, muttering something all the time, while Raisa had been bitterly crying with her head pressed into the pillow.

Early next morning Auntie went to Father Ivan, but he was already putting Raisa into an old tarantass; he coldly lectured Anna Mikhailovna on the immorality of her nephew, urged on his gelding and drove away with the broken brim of his hat flapping in the breeze.

Auntie went home, looking back occasionally at the departing tarantass, when she noticed Nikolushka emerge from under the dam and stand before them waving his cap. Father Ivan stood up and whipped his horse. Raisa would have leaned out of the carriage, but, held fast by the priest's hand, she covered her face with a handkerchief. All this excitement gave Auntie migraine.

Pushing the cold compress back from her eyes, Anna Mikhailovna began to speak in a weak voice:

"It is a sin to expect a reward from people, my friend, but still it hurts me—he is so very ungrateful. . . ."

"Hmm, that nephew of yours certainly likes taking the cream off the milk. . . ."

"Just think of it, he blames me for everything. . . . And Nastya is angry with me as though I had brought him and Raisa together."

"Give 'em both a sound thrashing—that's my opinion. . . ."

"Oh, no, anything but that, Afrikan Ilyich."

"And if they mustn't be thrashed, what then?"

"I can't imagine. . . . As soon as the priest comes back, go

44

to him, my friend, and tell him I want to confess and, if he allows it, I will take Holy Communion on Sunday."

Afrikan Ilyich groaned; he was an atheist but, out of respect for Auntie, he did not air his convictions. Anna Mikhailovna began to nod again. On the back porch Vasilisa was still singing the same monotonous song. It would have been better if there had been no such song in Christian Russia.

X

Two days passed. The Turenev house was calm but silent. They did not sit long at table but left immediately after meals for their respective rooms. In her kindly simplicity Anna Mikhailovna thought that Nikolushka's burst of passion had passed; Nikoluskha in fact walked about unshaven, gloomy and dejected, and it was only from Nastyenka's penetrating glances and her crooked smile that one could guess that all was not well with Nikolushka. . . .

Then this happened. Towards evening Nikolushka pulled a soft cap down to his ears, lit a cigarette and left the house. "Where are you going?" Auntie asked him. He shrugged his shoulders and answered, "Nowhere," and walked off across the dam to the mill. Afrikan Ilyich at that time was dozing in the box room, and there was nobody to tell Auntie what that "Nowhere" meant; she did not even recall that, half an hour before, she herself had sent Mashutka to the mill for some crayfish; which the miller's brother and the verger Konstantin Palych were catching with a dragnet in the millpond.

In the gully at the end of the dam stood the mill with its double-sloped, moss-covered roof. In the field behind the mill, stood some carts, from which the horses had been unharnessed, under the shade of huge crooked black poplars. Farther on the verger, his red hair fluttering in the wind and up to his knees in water, and the miller's brother, up to his chest in water, were moving slowly along near the low bank: they were pulling the dragnet and shouting: "How much deeper?" "Get in, I tell you!" "How much deeper, then?" "Get in, I tell you, antichrist. . . ."

Nikolushka walked slowly as far as the mill, went down to the spillway where a thin stream of water flowed over mildewed boards as slippery as silk; where the water wheel, black, wet and covered with the long green strands of waterweeds, groaned as it turned heavily and unwillingly; where in the greenish murk, which smelt of damp and tar, the wooden gears creaked and rattled as they turned, shaking the ramshackle old mill to its very foundations; where village boys, catching frogs with a cloth, had looked through the cracks between the boards of the staging and had often seen the water demon sitting on the bottom of the millpond with his webbed hands clasping the green piles. . . .

Nikolushka had nowhere in particular to go. He threw his cigarette butt into the foam under the mill wheel, climbed up the shaky ladder to where the dust from the flour swam in the sun's rays, where the heavy millstones flew lightly round and round, and the strong-smelling rye flour trickled into the hoppers; he picked up a pinch of flour, rubbed it between his fingers, and went out again beyond the gates.

Peasants, who had arrived before dawn with cartloads of grain to grind, sat out here in the field, some on the grass, others on a broken millstone. Assuming a stern look, Nikolushka greeted them in a deep voice: "Good-day, boys." Some of the peasants doffed their caps; Prov the miller, an old soldier, said invitingly, "Sit down, young master. . . ." and moved up, offering Nikolushka a place on the millstone. . . .

"That's how it was," Prov continued his story, pressing down the ashes in his pipe with a black finger, "there's no telling how many of our people he finished off. . . . General Baryatinsky would send out troops and Shamil finished them all off for him. . . . How many of our bones we left lying in that Caucasus, it's something terrible, boys. . . Shamil was stubborn, but General Baryatinsky was still more stubborn: 'you can't allow the Russian Emperor to retreat before Shamil', he said."

"Of course it made him sore," said one of the peasants, bending down and fiddling with the toe of his bast shoe.

"Well, yes, kind of sore. So General Baryatinsky gathered a big army and surrounded Shamil on all sides—he left him no food and no water; Shamil climbed right up to the top of a mountain with his Circassians and fired down from there, wouldn't surrender. . . . Our boys brought ladders and climbed and climbed, and, you know, as the first were killed others climbed in their places. . . . General Baryatinsky stood down below stroking his beard into two directions like this, and shouting: 'I will not permit Russian arms to be disgraced. . . .' "

"Some people are cocky that way," said the same peasant.

"At last the Circassians had no more shells left. That's when our troops got them. They reached the top of the hill and saw the Circassians standing round in a ring and Shamil sitting on a stone in the middle reading the Koran. 'Surrender!' the Russians shouted And what happened, brother? Just imagine, those Circassians, they got on their horses, wrapped their goatskin cloaks round them and jumped into the sea. . . . From that mountain it was eighteen versts down to the sea. . . . Just then our soldiers came up and grabbed Shamil and tied his hands. . . ."

"Still, the general had his own way." The same peasant said again.

Nikolushka sat on the millstone smoking and blinking frequently. The fact of the matter was that he had long ago noticed Mashutka nearby beside the carts. She was standing with her knee raised and her heel resting on the spoke of a wheel, looking cheerfully at Nikolushka. She was wearing a straight black blouse with yellow trimmings, the prevailing fashion of Turenevo village, a yellow kerchief and a red skirt.

"All right," said Nikolushka, frowning as though something were toward, "good-bye, boys!" He rose lazily and walked towards the carts, striding with his feet wide apart like a cavalryman.

Mashutka looked at him with laughing eyes. He pretended that he had only just noticed her and stopped in his tracks, swaying back and forth.

"Oh, you're here? What are you doing?"

Mashutka raised her eyebrows that seemed to have been finely drawn with charcoal, took her bare foot off the wheel and smiled.

"Auntie sent me for crayfish, and all those devils do is shout. They haven't caught a single one yet!"

She tossed her head and laughed out loud, jerking her elbow in the direction of the millpond.

"The verger doesn't want to go into the water, says he's a man of the church."

Nikolushka turned towards the wide pond that had taken on a bluish hue in the twilight. On the low bank, which had been stamped under the hoofs of the cattle, the verger and the miller's brother, a little, short peasant, were still bickering, dragging the net from each other. There was naturally nothing particular to laugh at in that foolish scene. Nikolushka wrinkled up his nose in disgust.

"And you just sit here," he said, pausing between his words. "Look out, or Auntie will be after you. Who are you waiting for?"

Mashutka's smiling face suddenly became serious and she pressed her lips together. She looked at Nikolushka attentively, almost sternly, her eyes shaded by long lashes, pulled her kerchief forward on to her forehead, walked away, stepping carefully with her bare feet, and then swiftly glanced back once more at Nikolushka.

"Oh, hell," he muttered, breathing in the air that had for some reason become particularly aromatic. "Oh, hell!"

The familiar pain of longing filled his breast. . . . It was becoming obvious—some force had got him out of bed earlier than usual that morning, had driven him from room to room, into the passage, the kitchen and the garden, and had finally brought him to the mill.

His feet grew light, his eyes became clearer: all the strength that was in him, all the sweet joy and the fire, was racing after the girl who was now walking away along the bank of the pond, the wind blowing out her red skirt and yellow kerchief. . . . When he had seen her standing by the wheel, that raised knee had turned Nikolushka's head—now the grass, yellowish-green in the light of the setting sun, was beating against her knees.

"To hell with Nastya and Auntie," he thought with divine nonchalance and followed the girl, his feet simply moving of their own accord across the meadow. She turned round, her little face with its black brows trembled in fear, and then walked faster: he ran. Panting, he caught up with her beside a stack of last year's straw near the threshing barns and seized her by the hand.

"Where are you running to?"

"Let me go, Nikolai Mikhailovich," she said in a quick whisper and twisted her arm, but her strength failed her.

"Listen, Masha, I want to talk to you about. . . ."

"Master, kind master, don't say it. . . ."

"It's like this. . . . I can't go on in this way any longer. . . . They have ruined my life. . . . I didn't sleep all last night. . . . I'll marry you, honestly, I will. . . "

"Master, dear master, they'll see us. . . ."

"They won't see anything. . . . Look how dark it's getting. . . . Sit down here, in the straw. . . . How pretty you are. . . . You didn't scratch your legs when you walked through the grass, did you? . . . What a lovely mouth. . . . What are you staring at me like that for, Masha, Mashenka. . . ."

Mashutka stared at Nikolushka's frightening, handsome smiling face, but saw nothing in her excitement; she seemed to hear him muttering something in the distance. She bit her lower lip to keep her chin from trembling. As she stared, she moved farther away trying to ward him off.

49

When Nikolushka ran along the bank of the pond after Mashutka, the peasants sitting by the mill were watching him.

"Ai, the young master's sticking his nose into our plate of soup," began one.

"And he's married too!"

"And what if he is. . . . They're worse when they're married; they're used to the sweets."

"He'll ruin the girl."

"Whose is she?"

"Vasilisa's, an orphan."

"A fine girl. . . ."

"D'you see how he flew after her?"

"He eats well, sleeps well, why shouldn't he be able to chase 'em?"

"Last year there was some sort of an artist came here and they broke his legs for him."

"It wouldn't hurt to break his. . . ."

"He's going towards the threshing barns. . . . Got his head screwed on all right. . . . He'll get her in the straw there and that'll be the end of it."

"There's no good in that business. . . ."

"Of course there's no good in it. . . ."

Two young Turenevo lads, who were lying on the grass nearby, stood up, glanced at each other, and then ran across the dam to the village. The peasants followed them with their eyes and said:

"They'll give him a beating. . . ."

"And what if they do? Nothing wrong in that. . . ."

"The young master will pay dear for his pleasure. . . ."

XI

At dusk Nastya sat by the dusty window of her bedroom. Her thin, cold hand held a fluffy brown shawl together at her throat—the shawl was a gift from Auntie who loved everything brown, of good quality and modest. Nastya was sleepy, but did not want to go to sleep; she felt as dull as the dusty

50

window with the dim outlines of the bushes, the tumbledown buildings with their collapsing thatched roofs and the barely visible washing on the line—a smudge of white in the twilight.

Auntie came in, her presence made known by the glow of her cigarette and sat down on a trunk near the wall.

"Don't you light the lamps?" she said softly.

"No . . . somehow I don't feel like it. . . ."

"Now, now!" She could hear Auntie stifling a yawn. "You are alone, Nastya?"

"Yes, alone. . . ."

"I'd noticed that Nikolushka was away a long time. He went away but I thought he had returned."

"He'll come."

Outside the window a grey cat stood up on its hind legs, stared through the window into the room, took away first one paw and then the other and disappeared. Nastya stirred in her chair.

"I don't like cats looking in at the window. . . . I had a friend once, a real coquette, she was so afraid of cats, she fainted. . . ."

"And Mashutka has disappeared somewhere too," said Auntie quickly.

"I used to live well once," Nastya began after a short pause. "I had my own apartment, furniture upholstered in blue satin, two fur coats—one sable and the other mink with ermine on top. And the diamonds I had! And that scoundrel squandered it all on drink. . . ."

"Oh, Nastyenka. . . ."

"Of course he's a scoundrel, the worst there is. . . ."

"Oh, Nastyenka. . . ."

"What, Anna Mikhailovna?"

"I think you should forgive him, Nastyenka. . . ."

"As though I had never forgiven him. . . . Oh, why did I come here? You should have seen the admirers I had. There was one baron who crawled before me on his knees, offered me a house on Sergiev Street, he brought me the title deed, and I threw him and his title deed out of the door because I couldn't stand him. . . . Forgive him. . . . I still have wounds on my body from his blows, but I forgave him. . . . And when he took my last necklace to the pawnshop I knew that I should never see a kopek of the money he got. . . . He pawned the necklace and drank the money with my friend Sonka Yevrion, the coquette. . . . I scratched the skin off his ugly mug—and I forgave him. . . . I would have followed him to hard labor if he had loved me alone and no other. . . ."

Nastyenka stopped, sniffed, and began to fumble for a handkerchief in the armchair in which she was sitting.

"You had better talk to him about the forgiveness, Anna Mikhailovna. . . . All he thinks of now is how to get his revenge on me, because I got him away from that bit of a girl, that Raisa. . . . I know who he's got on his brain now: he's making up to your Mashutka. . . ."

"God alone knows what you are saying!" exclaimed Auntie and got up from the trunk. "Excuse me, Nastyenka, but you have a very wicked imagination. . . . I have been watching you for some time. . . . it is hard, hard, with you. . . ."

Nastya sobbed and threw herself into the depths of the big armchair. Strangely enough, her face seemed to grow brighter, rosier. Her fine profile stood out more clearly against the brown of the old upholstery and a fantastic light turned her hair to gold until her whole head with its closed eyes was lit up. . . .

"What's that?" exclaimed Auntie. "What a light!"

Nastya opened her eyes and gasped: the window was like a crimson rectangle in the plastered wall.

"Fire!" she screamed, jumping out of the chair.

Silently Auntie raised her hands to her head. Doors were already slamming in the house, there was a trampling of feet and frightened voices calling for Auntie. The door opened with a crash, a draught blew across the room, and Afrikan Ilyich came in.

"Fire!" he said in a thick voice. "They have set fire to the threshing barns!"

52

He stood at the window and watched the red glow, his hands folded behind his back, round-shouldered and red-faced. Nastya lay down on the bed and buried her face in the pillow.

Auntie shouted down the passage.

"Nikolushka! Where is Nikolushka? Girls, girls, run and find the young master."

The glow grew brighter. The log walls of the outhouses in the yard were all lit up. Thick dancing shadows sprang from the bushes, the curious idlers standing at the gates made black silhouettes. . . . They heard frightened voices calling.

"He's coming. . . . He's coming. . . ."

One of the girls ran into the house and whispered loudly down the passage.

"Mistress, he's come!"

Auntie hurried to meet him and suddenly exclaimed in a horrified voice:

"Oh, my Lord! . . ."

Afrikan Ilyich turned away from the window. Nastya lifted her head from the pillow. Nikolushka came in, hatless, disheveled, his shirt showing white under his arm where his coat was torn. His mouth was black and battered, one eye and cheek were swollen. . . . With his elbow he pushed aside Auntie, who had come mincing up to him, and collapsed on to a chair.

"Send them all to court! Shoot them!" he screamed and, bending over, began spitting blood on the floor.

Auntie was already beside him with a towel and a jug of water; Nastya sat bolt upright on the bed, her neck stretched out, and stared penetratingly at Nikolushka with horror-stricken eyes.

"Calm down, calm down, my friend," muttered Auntie, laying the wet towel on Nikolushka's face. "To think that such a thing should happen. . . . Who did this to you?"

"I gave one of them what he asked for, straight in the teeth!"

"All right, all right, calm down, young man!"

Afrikan Ilyich, his feet apart, his hands in his pockets, was looking Nikolushka up and down.

"Tell us where they did this to you?" he asked. "You must have been in the barn. You have straw in your hair. . . ."

Leaning over to him he asked softly but sternly:

"Did you see Masha?"

"She ran away," answered Nikolushka, "she escaped. . . ."

Afrikan Ilyich glanced swiftly at Auntie whose cheeks and chin shook angrily. Nastya, smiling strangely, slid down from the bed and, squatting in front of Nikolushka, spoke to him in a wheedling, almost gay tone.

"Tell us, Koka, tell us, how were things with you and her."

The barns were still burning when Afrikan Ilyich went out into the garden. A thin smoke spread over the damp grass, the trunks of the birches glowed red, here and there a wet leaf glistened, dark red shadows hovered across the meadow and the dry crown of the poplar stood out clearly against the sky.

The old house, gazing with its blood-red windows into the smoky meadows looked as if it had been lifted partly out of a mass of dark thickets; it had come to life, gloomy, majestic, and solemn, with its six peeling plastered columns, and its tumbledown fronton above which rose-lit doves whirled in the glow of the fire.

On the second floor Afrikan Ilyich saw a pale white face pressed for a minute against one of the windows and then withdraw. Afrikan Ilyich ascended to the balcony, opened the door which stood half ajar and entered the drawing room; the black silhouettes of leaves and branches lay on the bare plaster walls like Chinese paintings; he listened and then walked on from room to room up to his knees in grain.

In the library, where the old books were still lying round the stepladder, where the glass doors and their brass corners glistened, he saw Mashutka hiding in a corner behind a black bookcase—her head was bare, she stood with her head drawn into her shoulders like a cornered rat. Afrikan Ilyich took her by the hand. She screamed weakly and broke away. He seized her more firmly and took her downstairs to Auntie.

XII

When Anna Mikhailovna saw Mashutka in her bedroom, disheveled, with head hanging down, her face began to twitch; she rolled her eyes, sat down on the floor and began to moan —a heart attack had begun. Next morning there came another attack and they sent for the village doctor. The whole house became quiet. Afrikan Ilyich, black as a thundercloud, walked about in his socks. Mashutka, who had been severely thrashed by Vasilisa, was hiding in one of the many big, dusty store-rooms of the Turenev house. Nikolushka lay in bed with his head covered and refused both food nor drink. Nastya wandered about not knowing what to do: she looked haggard, her nose had become more pointed and she seemed to be burning up inside, as though consumed with an inner fire.

On the third day Auntie felt better. Father Ivan came to see her and spent some hours in conversation with her although nobody knew what they were talking about. In the evening, Afrikan Ilyich went into Nikolushka's room and stood there a minute in silence while he rolled himself a cigarette and slowly lit it.

"Take the trouble to get up immediately, dress yourself and go to Anna Mikhailovna in her bedroom," he said.

Nikolushka groaned softly under the blanket, but he got up, dressed himself and, scarcely able to drag his legs, supporting himself by the walls, made his way to Auntie; and when she gave him permission to sit down, he lowered himself on a chair near the door, dropped his head and, like one in torment, closed his eyes surrounded with purple bruises. Afrikan Ilyich sat on Auntie's bed and smoked, screwing up his eyes at the smoke. Auntie sat in her armchair, round-shouldered, wrinkled, scarcely alive. . . .

"Firstly," she said, her voice scarcely audible from weakness but quite firm, "be kind enough to tell me all. . . . First, you must admit everything frankly. . . ."

Nikolushka began to rock to and fro on his chair, and for a long time could not say a word: he just bellowed like a cow and, then, having found the right line, he began to tell them how his whole life had been nothing but struggle and tragedy; he dreamed of self-perfection, of stern and honest labor, but all manner of contingencies had arisen and had again and again pushed him into the abyss. His blood grew cold, his soul slumbered in despair, and he strove hungrily towards a bright, pure light, which would fire his blood, awaken him to activity. . . . Every time, however, that tiny light had turned out to be a temptation of the devil. . . . The day before yesterday, for example, he had gone to the carts in order to order Mashutka home and make her stop hanging idly about. . . . And that girl, instead of obeying him, had looked at him so archly, had raised her knee on the wheel, and instantly the abyss had opened before him. . . .

"Auntie," he exclaimed, beating his breast and falling on his knees, "surely you must understand the depths of degradation people have led me to! . . . Hold out your hand to me, lift me out of the abyss. . . ."

Anna Mikhailovna listened, her nose down, her eyes closed; and from under her wrinkled eyelids, there trickled occasional and evidently bitter tears. . . .

Afrikan Ilyich coughed several times to encourage Auntie. Mastering her excitement and sorrow, she said to Nikolushka:

"Go back to your room!"

He bowed and, as he was in a mood conversation, knocked at Nastya's door and talked with her till dawn. The floor boards creaked under his feet the whole night long and his dull, velvety voice could be heard throughout the silent Turenev house. Upstairs, where the grain lay, the mice squeaked and scampered all night. All night the window in Anna Mikhailovna's room shone through the bushes: kneeling before the miraculous Redeemer she prayed that the Lord bring light into the desolate gloom of that ancient, sinful house.

Next morning Nikolushka came down to breakfast refreshed—all the black spots on his soul had been cleansed and washed away during the night. Nastya came down, sad, tired and silent. Afrikan Ilyich looked at them and groaned, turned his back on them and continued drinking tea from his saucer. Nikolushka asked him for some tobacco and he pushed the tobacco box across to him with his elbow. Nastya, who was pouring out tea, laughed.

"Smoking is an expensive and unhealthy habit," said Nikolushka. "I'm thinking of giving it up."

At that moment Auntie came into the dining room in a black hat, shapeless from its long stay in a trunk: it was fastened with ribbons under her chin and sat on her head like a bonnet. Looking into the corner she said:

"Nikolai, get ready, we're leaving. . . ."

The saucer trembled in Nikolushka's hand and he spilt his tea.

"Where to, Auntie?"

"To the monastery," answered Auntie firmly; and taking Afrikan Ilyich by the sleeve, she led him aside to talk to him in secret.

Nastya sat silent, her grey eyes wide open. Nikolushka traced patterns on the wet oilcloth with his finger. . . .

"Take only the most essential things with you, we'll talk on the way," Auntie said and sat down to the table to drink a cup of tea before leaving.

An hour later Auntie and Nikolushka were seated in the tarantass, on cushions embroidered in cross-stitch. Nikolushka, his cap askew, was smiling pitifully; he waved his hand to Nastya for the last time.

"Good-bye, sweetheart!"

Nastya stood on the porch, her mouth half covered with the fluffy shawl, either crying or laughing.

"God be with you!" exclaimed Auntie.

The horses moved off. A hound ran out from under the tarantass. A frightened chicken ran clucking from the road. They were off.

Nastyenka came out and sat on the steps of the porch, leaning her arms on her knees, her hands supporting her chin. In the deep blue sky over the Turenev Manor House, over the road where the tarantass came into sight again at the bend, over the dwindling family woods—white clouds floated indifferently.

Afrikan Ilyich, leaning against the post of the porch, smoked and sighed deeply. Suddenly one of his eyes—it hung low like that of a dog—winked.

"Ai, ai, they've packed that cockerel off!"

MISHKA NALYMOV
A TALE OF THE TRANS-VOLGA

I

The manor houses of the gentry of Stavropol Uyezd have for centuries occupied the low-lying land beyond the Volga; they stand in the shade of grey gardens laid out around ponds and swimming pools; thatched barns and other farm buildings stood in extensive farmyards overgrown with grass.

The traveler seated in a tarantass on cushions embroidered in all four corners with cockerels, his equipage drawn by two sorry, fly-tormented post nags, had no reason for raising his weary eyelids; heat, dusty road that wound its way imperceptibly across the steppes, larks high up in the heavens over the cornfields and, far away in the distance, thatched roofs and long poles over the wells. . . . Sometimes the crowns of willows rose above low hills and, occasionally, a tarantass would roll past a low pond whose banks were pitted with the hoofmarks of cattle, past a ditch thickly overgrown with acacia, past the house of the Nalymov family, the pillars of which gleamed white through the green of the poplars.

In this case, a traveler who knew the local customs would turn his horses directly off the road so as to avoid the manor house and grounds, especially if Mishuka—Mikhal Mikhalych Nalymov—were sitting at the window in his dressing gown. Mishuka had long, drooping mustaches, three folds of flesh that lay in waves on the nape of his bull neck, and he would sit and frown grimly at any passing tarantass.

No one knew what to expect from Mishuka: he might order his servants to run after a traveler and invite him into the house, would unharness the horses and send them out grazing with his own herds and roll the tarantass into the pond so that the wood should not dry out and crack. Or else, if a traveler did not take his fancy, he would rage and fume, lean out of the window, and scream: "Let loose the dogs—this is my land, how dare you drive past the house, you accursed devils! . . ." And the Nalymov dogs—it were better not to see them even in a dream. In winter he had another trick—he would order the traveler to be stopped and given a besom to sweep away the traces left by his sleigh. Like it or not, he would have to get out of the sleigh and sweep while the dogs sat nearby with the hoarfrost gleaming white on their whiskers.

Anybody who knew the customs of the place, then, would make a wide detour in the steppes in order to avoid the Nalymov house. Guests came there rarely, but this was for a different reason.

One afternoon Mishuka was sitting at his open window as usual. The carriage house at the far end of the grass-grown yard stood with its doors wide open and grooms were going in and out. Suddenly they stepped aside to make way for a light open carriage to which three bays were harnessed; it came flying out of the carriage house as though released from a spring, described a semicirle and pulled up at the porch so suddenly that the trace horses sat back on their rumps while the shaft horse tossed its head and dug its hoofs deep into the soft ground. The coachman, dressed in a black waistcoat and a crimson shirt, took off a glove whitened with chalk, closed one of his nostrils by pressing his thumb against it and blew his nose on to the ground. A groom who had run all the way from the carriage house took the shaft horse by the bridle.

Mishuka leaned out of the window and examined the horses —a magnificent team, splendid beasts. Pleased with the sight, he got up from his chair, went into the next room and shouted: "Vanyushka!" A heavy-jowled boy came into the room. Mishuka sat down on the wooden bed and held out, first, one fat leg and, then, the other to the boy who pulled wide panta-loons on to them; Mishuka changed his dressing gown for a

60

linen jacket, took up a short stock whip and a white peaked cap with red piping, threw out his broad chest and, treading heavily on the bare boards, went out on to the porch.

The shaft horse turned and gave a short neigh of pleasure when it saw Mishuka. Pyotr Ilyich, the estate steward, dressed in a long-tailed green coat, came up to his master and reported to him respectfully.

"Your Excellency," he said, "Miss Maria and Miss Dunya and Miss Telipatra ordered horses this morning, but I did not let them have any."

Mishuka walked down the porch steps with his legs wide apart and stood looking up at the attic windows where the curtains were still drawn. He stood looking at the windows for a long time, shook his whip at them and stroked his mustaches.

"No horses are to be given to anybody without my permission, the accursed devils," he said and walked towards the carriage.

"Yes, sir. . . . And then the gardener came to the office complaining that Miss Fimka and Miss Bronka were picking raspberries, they stripped the canes. . . ."

"Oh, hell," exclaimed Mishuka, turning red, "I'll give it to them. . . ."

He pondered a moment, climbed into the carriage which tipped towards him under his weight, dropped heavily on the spring cushions, and pushed his peaked cap down over his eyes. The coachman took up the reins and turned his head.

"To Repievka!" Mishuka ordered but as the carriage moved off he shouted: "Stop!"

"Hi, Pyotr Ilyich, call them all down here. Hurry!"

The steward ran into the house. Soon the girls, arranging their shawls and dressing gowns as they came out, appeared on the porch—Cleopatra tall and thin, Maria, scared, sloppy and untidy, her bare feet thrust into her shoes, pretty Dunya leaning against a pillar behind them and gazing indifferently at the sky, and Fimka and Bronka, the village wenches, who were huddled together in the doorway staring at Mishuka with their noses wrinkled. . . .

"You," said Mishuka, blowing out his ginger mustaches, "look out for yourselves. I'm going away for three days and if any of you. . . ."—he slapped his whip against the leg of his boot—"see to it that not one of you . . . anything. . . ."

"Yes, that's all we need," Cleopatra said, twisting her mouth.

Pretty Dunya shrugged her shoulders lazily and looked up at the sky.

"Bring us some sweets," she said.

Mishuka frowned, wheezed, wanted to say something, but changed his mind and shouted to the coachman: "Get on!" and away they went.

As Mishuka drove along the road gazing at the fields of rye and wheat that stretched on either side as far as the horizon, he wiped his florid face from time to time with a handkerchief; he was not thinking about anything in particular.

One of the minor landed gentry passed him in a droshky. Mishuka placed two fingers to his cap and looked sternly, his light eyes bulging out of his head, at the gentleman who greeted him deferentially.

They crossed a gully where they almost broke their springs in a pothole; they were all splashed with mud and, by the time they reached the top, the trace horses were in a lather; from there the road ran between mown meadows and a breeze sprang up.

"Repiev's," said the coachman, pointing with his whip to where a long droshky drawn by a pair was rolling along a country lane. A red sunshade bobbed over the white shirts of the people in the droshky. When Mishuka's troika drew abreast the droshky, its occupants shouted to him.

"Uncle Misha, come over to our place, come and see us!"

Between the two young Repiev brothers, Nikita and Sergei, sat a tall, young girl with fair hair. She held a red parasol in her hand, her straw hat was pushed back on to her neck where it hung by a ribbon, her light laughing eyes met Mishuka's goggle-eyed stare. He removed his cap and bowed. The carriage had moved on far ahead, but Mishuka was still thinking —Who is she? Who can it be?" In his slowly-working mind he went over all the Repiev relations.

"It can't be anybody but Vera Khodanskaya, that's who it is!"

He was still turning it over in his mind, gazing from one side to the other, when the huge Repiev garden appeared from behind a hill and, in the distance, the rippling Volga glistened like fish scales in the sunlight.

II

The elder Repievs, brother and sister, were sitting on a balcony shaded by lilacs; they sat facing the garden and the ponds.

Olga Leontievna, in a lace boudoir cap and wearing round spectacles, with lips compressed, was embroidering a runner for the tea table; Pyotr Leontievich, her brother, who as usual was wearing just a black waistcoat, sat in silence, screwing up one eye and looking slyly at his sister with the other, all the time tapping on the floor with a boot whose walrus-hide top he loved pulling up. At such times he would say: "Look, I've been wearing them for twenty years and they're still as good as new." He wore a velvet skullcap, and the breeze played in his grey beard and the sleeves of his white shirt.

"I don't know how it's all going to end," said Olga Leontievna.

"How what'll end, Olenka?"

Olga Leontievna looked at him over the top of her glasses.

"You know very well what I'm worrying about."

"About Vera? Yes, yes, I'm thinking about Vera, too." Pyotr Leontievich, leaning on the arms of his chair, half rose and seated himself more comfortably. "Yes, it's quite a problem."

"Stop tapping your foot," Olga Leontievna said to him.

Her brother tapped a couple of times more and then screwed up both eyes.

"I think Seryozha ought to go away for a while," he said, pulling at the leg of his boot.

"Oh, Pyotr, I've known that for a long time without your help. . . . But it's a much more difficult business than that, you mark my words. . . ."

"Not really?!"

"No, not that, you ought to be ashamed of yourself, Pyotr. . . . But still, it's much, much more complicated than it seems. . . ."

Brother and sister sat in silence. The birds were singing in the garden. The leaves were rustling. . . . It was warm and quiet for the old people, sitting there on the balcony. The sound of a bell came from the distance.

"Whose bell could that be?" asked Pyotr Leontievich.

Olga Leontievna took off her glasses and listened.

"That's Nalymov's bell. Surely it can't be Mishuka? What wind has blown him here?"

Mishuka, entering the balcony from the garden, bent over Olga Leontievna's hand, kissed Pyotr Leontievich, thinking the while, "The old man still kisses even if his estate is ruined —the damned old liberal."

Mishuka took off his cap and sat down, wiping his face and bald head with a handkerchief. Pyotr Leontievich, smiling, tapped him on the knee. Olga Leontievna continued her embroidery and spoke to him in a tone that was not exactly approving.

"It's a long time since you were here, Mishenka."

"I've been busy with the elections to the Zemstvo."

"Oh, I see," with a sidelong glance at her brother, "you sent the peasants packing again."

"Yes, we blackballed them." Mishuka turned with a frown towards the garden. "This is no time to elect them, treasonable times, these are. . . ."

64

"I've been wanting to give you a piece of my mind for a long time," Olga Leontievna began after a pause; "it is unworthy of a gentleman to play the pranks you do, Mishenka."

"What pranks?"

"Like that one not so long ago when you brought some shopkeeper to a hotel in Simbirsk, made him drunk, won all his money at cards, and then threw him out of the room —what's more, he went head first through the door and the door was smashed."

"Oh, that's when I treated what's his name, Vaska Sevryugin. . . ."

"Good heavens, what difference does it make if it was Vaska Sevryugin . . . and they couldn't bring him round for three days. . . . Foul, Mishenka, unworthy. . . ."

"Sevryugin was going to the toilet in the early morning," Mishuka said, "when he saw a lackey in the corridor without his coat on—he was cleaning windows. . . . 'What,' he says to the lackey, 'you dare appear before me without a coat,' and began to beat him up. Years ago that lackey, Yevdokim, worked for my father as an errand boy, he remembers us all, he's a man to respect. Sevryugin came back from the toilet to my room and told me how he had beaten up Yevdokim. . . . 'You understand,' he says, 'I'm a cloth manufacturer.' And I said to him: 'You're a swine, I'll turn you into calico. . . .' He took offence, I pushed him and he went through the door. That's all."

Mishuka spent a long time wiping himself with his handkerchief after such a long speech while Olga Leontievna, laying down her embroidery, could not refrain from laughing; her face became a mass of wrinkles and she shook all over as old people do.

Vera ran out of the garden on to the balcony; behind her came Sergei, taking the stairs three at a time; and last of all came Nikita, smiling bashfully and kindheartedly. Vera held

65

out both her hands to Mishuka and looked at him gaily with her grey flashing eyes.

"Let me introduce myself, Uncle Misha. Do you remember how you used to push me on the swing?"

"Why yes, I think I remember." Mishuka got up with great difficulty. "Of course, you're Verochka. . . . Yes, yes, I remember the swing, I remember it quite well now. . . ."

He bent his head to one side. His bear's eyes became quite round. Vera looked into them and suddenly blushed. Her face looked sweet and confused. That lasted only a moment, however, before she lifted her dress slightly and curtseyed gravely.

"You may congratulate me," she said, "I am nineteen tomorrow. . . ."

Pyotr Leontievich, glancing at Vera with a smile of pleasure, nudged his sister with his elbow and chuckled. Nikita held up his hand to his ear.

"What? What did she say?" he asked.

"I said that tomorrow I shall be an old maid. It is an occasion on which we shall have guests, we shall go boating. . . ."

"Yes, of course, we shall go boating," repeated Nikita and nodded his head.

Vera sat on the balustrade, put her arm round a white pillar and leaned her temple against it. Sergei, dark, with an aquiline nose and bright but malicious eyes, stood beside Vera with one hand thrust into his leather belt. Nikita made several attempts to approach her, then retreated, and finally dropped his pince-nez. Mishuka, looking at the young people, began roaring with laughter.

"You know what?" Olga Leontievna said, rising from her chair, "let's go and have tea."

Nikita dallied on the balcony. He stood beside the pillar wiping his pince-nez and still smiling in his confusion; then his face became sad—in general he was a little out of place—in his pongee jacket, check trousers, a carefully washed look about him, absent-minded and awkward.

Vera turned round to look at him as she reached the door, then came back and stood beside him.

"Nikita, I am very sad, do you know why?"

"What did you say?"

"I said I am sad," she took hold of the top button on his waistcoat and he blushed, smiling pitifully.

"No, Verochka, I don't know why."

"Why are you blushing?"

"I'm not blushing, it's only your fancy."

Vera raised her clear eyes and looked at the clouds, her face was clear cut and refined and on her throat there was a little dimple that throbbed as she breathed.

"All right, it was just a fancy," she sang rather than said.

"Verochka, do you like Sergei very much?" Nikita asked, a whole minute later.

"Of course I do and I like you too."

Nikita pressed her hand softly, but his lips trembled and he did not dare look her in the face. Sergei appeared in the doorway, chewing a cheesecake.

"Oh, a sentimental interlude!" he guffawed. "I was told to call you in to tea. . . ."

III

The boats floated along by the reeds under the willows. In the leading boat sat Vera, Sergei and Mishuka, who was rowing, plunging the oars, heavy from waterweeds, deeply into the water. Looking at Vera from under his wet eyebrows, Mishuka wheezed and thought to himself that there he was —rowing, humiliating himself on account of a chit of a girl.

"It's hot," he said, wiping his mustache.

"Uncle Misha, let me take the oars." Vera rose, the boat began to rock, and the people in the other boat shouted to her: "Vera, Vera, you'll fall!"

A frightened duck quacked in the reeds.

"No, I began rowing and I'll continue," Mishuka said. He liked Vera's legs in their openwork stockings and he liked the lace on her uplifted petticoats. "She's a hell of a fine girl," he thought. "An adopted child, the devil take it, no mother or father, in a hurry to get married . . . the devil take it."

Sergei sat with his legs tucked up under him, his aquiline-nosed face bent towards his shoulder, playing a mandolin. His cunning black eyes were gleaming gaily, as he stared at the water with narrowed eyes and seemed to avoid looking at Vera. The sun was going to rest, but it was still hot. The down from the lime trees fluttered about and settled on the mirrorlike surface of the water. For some time two dragon-flies, linked together, buzzed over Mishuka's head.

Far away in a summerhouse, whose six columns were reflected in the water, sat Nikita.

"Nika," Vera called out loudly across the water, "is tea ready?" Under Mishuka's glance, however, she immediately turned red as she had done the day before and knitted her brows slightly.

"You have a very pretty voice, Vera," Sergei said strumming on his mandolin, "really, you have, it's very pretty. . . ."

Vera flushed a still deeper red and bit her lips. Mishuka smirked.

Their boat was overtaken by the other which was being steered by Auntie Osorgina, who never rode in a carriage for fear of breaking the springs. She was dressed in a wide-cut lilac-colored dress, a lace cap and gloves, and gazed sternly from under her heavy brows at Nounou, Chouchou and Bébé, her three daughters, who were rowing.

Nounou, small and plump, gave a sudden sob because she could not drag the heavy oars out of the waterweeds. Chou-chou, who was thin and had a long red nose, was bad-tempered by nature. Bébé, the youngest, who still wore her hair down although she was over twenty, rowed clumsily and capriciously, knowing that she was pretty—in the family she was considered beautiful and called "capricious".

As they rowed past Auntie Osorgina said in a chesty bass: "Yes, young lady, it's time to eat and drink."

The boats rowed over to the summerhouse where Nikita

sat, his cheek resting on his hand, at a tea table covered with a white cloth and set with blue china tea things.

The Misses Osorgina, with tiny squeaks and screams, raised their dresses and stepped ashore followed by their dignified mother; Vera and Sergei jumped out, and Mishuka climbed heavily to the summerhouse making the stairs creak under his weight.

Vera sat down at the samovar. Her beautiful arms, bare to the elbow (Mishuka could not take his eyes off them), looked fresh and fragrant, like the tea she was pouring. Auntie Osorgina seated her three daughters by her side according to their ages.

"Two cups of tea with milk each and a piece of bread and butter," she ordered in her deep bass.

"A delightful pond, so romantic," Bébé said and threw her plaited hair over her shoulder.

"Our pond is better than this, but we have no boats," Chouchou said. "Our garden is better too."

Nounou sat silent and sad, but ate heartily of her bread and butter until her mother said "Refrain!" to her.

Nikita sat apart from the others, silently adjusting his pince-nez and smiling into his teacup. Sergei had again taken up his mandolin. Vera handed him a plate of raspberries.

"You offended me in the boat," she whispered, "ask my pardon."

"Your lips are so close, I'll kiss you in a minute," whispered Sergei just as quickly and without looking up.

Mishuka suddenly raised the alarm.

"Either you whisper or you don't. If you whisper, then let us all whisper. . . ."

The Misses Osorgina giggled. Verra flushed a deep red and her moist eyes sparkled.

From behind the dark lime trees there rose the red line of a rocket which burst into a shower of stars. It spluttered out with a gasp in the air and scared the rooks nested in the willows.

"Beautiful illuminations! Come along, let us have a good look at them," Auntie Osorgina said and led the way along the sagging boardwalk to the bank of the pond.

Everybody left the summerhouse. Its round roof and six peeling columns were now dimly reflected in the pond's dark waters faintly tinged with orange. It seemed better and more beautiful in the water, exactly as one of the Repiev ancestors had wished it to look when he built it in memory of his wife who had died young. Carpenters from Galicia had hewn it out of the trees the dead woman loved and had plastered and painted it with Greek designs. In the middle was a plaster cupid, holding with one hand a lowered torch while with the other covering her weeping eyes. Over the entrance was an inscription, now almost rubbed away:

> *"Friend of my lifetime, gone, alas,*
> *All earthly things so swiftly pass . . .*
> *Soon I'll be there where thou now art*
> *So wait in peace for me, dear heart."*

Every evening great-grandfather Repiev would sit in this summerhouse alone with his thoughts and memories, whispering the name of his dear, departed companion. One autumn, when the pond was covered with fallen leaves, when a mist spread over the reeds and the ducks were flying away into the sorrowful glow of the setting sun, great-grandfather Repiev disappeared. He was found later with boat hooks, lying amongst the waterweeds at the bottom of the pond.

The multi-colored lanterns were dying down amidst the damp foliage of the lime trees in the avenue. The yellowish moon could be seen through the branches hanging low over the garden. Girls from the village stood about in groups amongst the trees. They had just finished an old song which they had sung at Olga Leontievna's request and were now chewing sunflower seeds and using their elbows to fend off the village lads.

70

A Tartar fiddler was sitting on the ground, playing a sad, wild song of the steppes and rocking his shaved head with its skullcap back and forth. Olga Leontievna, Pyotr Leontievich, Osorgina and Chouchou, sat listening to the Tartar playing. The others had gone to dress up. To everybody's astonishment, Mishuka had gone with them.

"I don't like Mishuka today," Olga Leontievna whispered to her brother.

A shower of sparks came from the bushes, a rocket hissed, wound its way into the dark sky and burst high overhead. . . . The Tartar stopped sawing with his bow and, together with the girls and the guests, followed the rocket.

"How beautiful that was," Olga Leontievna sighed as the rocket gave its dying gasp.

At last the party appeared in costume: Vera, in a Turkish shawl and an old nightcap, represented a Turkish girl, Bébé a fishergirl with her hair in a net and an oar in her hand, Nounou, as "Night", wore a long black veil, while Nikita, who kept adjusting his pince-nez all the time, was dressed as a coachman. Mishuka simply had a bedsheet thrown over his head. . . .

"I don't know what costume that is supposed to represent," Olga Leontievna said pointing to Mishuka.

Auntie Osorgina took a lorgnette from her bag and looked at him.

"That is a ghost," she said.

The Tartar played a Polish dance. Vera whirled round with Nikita, Nounou with Bébé, and Mishuka remained alone, stamping his feet like a goose. A lantern amongst the branches caught fire and fell to the ground.

Suddenly a devil, dressed in a sheepskin, his face blackened with soot, leaped out of the bushes at the village girls. He leaped around just like a real devil, seized the beautiful, but desperately howling Vasyonka and began to dance and whirl round with her. . . .

Vera left Nikita and, fanning herself briskly, stood staring smilingly as Sergei, who was playing the devil, and at Vasyonka. Mishuka came closer to Vera.

"In my opinion, that's a bit too much," he boomed in her ear. "There's nothing funny about it and it's undignified. . . ."

Vera did not listen to him, but went up to Vasyonka, who was puffing and panting as she straightened her shawl; she took Vasyonka by the face, looked into her eyes, kissed them, and then kissed her on the cheek.

"How pretty you are, Vasyonka."

Vasyonka broke away from her and ran laughing to hide behind the other girls.

Osorgina shook her head disapprovingly. The Misses Osorgina were whispering like aspen leaves. Olga Leontievna rose and invited the guests into the house to supper.

"Come on, Uncle Misha," Vera said suddenly to Mishuka.

She took him under the arm and led him across a glade damp and silver-grey in the moonlight; she took him to a bench and sat down.

"It is stuffy under the limes. . . ."

"It's stuffy, yes," said Mishuka.

Vera leaned her head on his shoulder.

"Oh, Uncle Misha. . . ."

"What?"

"I only said 'Oh'. . . ."

"Vera?" wheezed Mishuka cautiously.

"What, Uncle Misha?"

He looked long at her delicate profile, pale in the moonlight and moved closer to her.

"What do you think of me?" he wheezed.

"I like you, Uncle Misha. . . ."

Mishuka did not answer, but clasped her in a bearlike grasp, stuck out his lips till he looked terrible and buried his lips and mustache in her neck, below her ear. . . .

"Let's go to my house. To hell with them all! We'll get married. Listen, let's go."

Silently, looking him straight in the face, Vera struggled,

72

scratched him till her nails broke, tore herself loose and, drawing on her cap and shawl, ran across the grass to the centre of the glade. Mishuka ran after her.

"You're mad," she cried, pressing her hands to her breast.

From the shadow behind a hedge of lilacs came Nikita. Mishuka stopped, turned sharply round, and went back into the depths of the garden. Vera ran up to Nikita.

"Please take me back home. I am quite giddy, I don't know what from."

Nikita took Vera by the arm, walked a few steps, and then said in a stammering whisper:

"I saw it, Vera. . . ."

Her arm suddenly became heavy. Vera turned round and then raised her face to his. In the moonlight he saw the tears running down her cheeks.

IV

Everybody left the garden except a few of the village girls who sat closely together on the grass in the linden avenue, whispering and laughing softly. There were still three Chinese lanterns burning in the branches. The moon stood high in the heavens. Sergei, laying his sooty face on Vasyonka's knee, was telling terrifying stories. The girls nudged each other, gasped in fright and giggled. . . .

"So Granddad Repiev sat at night in the summerhouse," Sergei continued in a low voice—Vasyonka's hand lay on his head and she stroked his hair or ran her fingers through it— "and there he sat and sat until suddenly he saw somebody coming towards him, walking across the water. . . ."

"Oh!"

"Vasyonka, did you nudge me?"

"Who's that touching me?"

"Keep quiet, girls!"

"She came on towards him, walking on the water, and Granddad grew afraid. He cringed into the corner of the summerhouse and dared not move. . . . It was a moonlit night just like it is now. . . . The thing, the white thing, came nearer and nearer on the water. It stopped outside the summerhouse. Then Granddad saw that it was his dead wife coming to him. . . ."

"Oh, I'm scared."

"Who is that keeps touching me?"

"Oh, stop it, you girls. . . ."

"Well, he shouldn't have looked at her, he should have closed his eyes. But he looked. Grandma smiled and pointed to her eyes with her finger. Granddad got up from the bench and went towards her. . . . He went out of the summerhouse, down the steps into the water. And Grandma laughed, beckoning him on as she flew over the water. . . . Granddad went in up to his waist and still she beckoned him on. The water was already up to Granddad's neck, but still he followed her. Ahead of him was a whirlpool. Granddad began to swim, he wanted to catch her. But Grandma bent over him and then disappeared with him under the water into the depths where there are great whiskered salmon. . . ."

The girls pressed close against each other.

"Sergei!" a voice suddenly called from amongst the bushes. The girls groaned softly in fright. Sergei raised his head.

"What do you want, Nikita?"

"I want you, please."

"I'll come in a minute."

"D'you know, there's been an unpleasant incident."

"Another incident."

Sergei unwillingly rose from the ground, jumped over the girls' legs and went towards the pond after Nikita.

"Oh, that Nalymov," Sergei said, laughing, when he heard the whole story. "Oh, that Mishuka. We must give him a lesson. Where is he now?"

"I think he's in the summerhouse. He went to Vera's window and called to her to come out and talk to him. He is sure she will come."

Nikita was slightly out of breath as he hurried after Sergei who strode rapidly across the wet grass. The moonlight flecked

74

the black pond with spots of gold. Nalymov's white jacket showed up clearly in the summerhouse.

Sitting in the summerhouse, Mishuka was thinking that he was not a bit afraid of the old Repievs, nevertheless he felt ill at ease.

"Two dogs after the same bitch," he thought. "So she wags her tail. . . . I can scratch, too. . . . The foundling—she ought to be grateful—if I marry her. . . . And this is what I'll give Seryozhka and Nikita. . . ."

Mishuka looked gloomily at his hairy fist. Just then voices became audible, the bushes were pushed apart and he saw Nikita's white jacket on the glade in front of the summerhouse; Sergei strode rapidly and insolently beside Nikita, his face as black as a devil's. . . .

Mishuka rapidly counted up to ten and assumed that, if Sergei did not reach the boardwalk by that time, everything would be all right. Sergei did get there. Mishuka gulped.

"I want to know what it's all about," Sergei said impudently, standing in front of him.

"What's all what about?"

"I'm asking you: what is the meaning of your impudence to Vera?"

Nikita nodded his head sympathetically: yes, yes. . . .

"Get to hell out of here, d'you hear me," answered Mishuka.

"With the greatest pleasure. But, as a preliminary, you and I have some shooting to do."

"What?" Mishuka got up.

Sergei struck him across the cheek and Mishuka sat down again, wheezing horribly; he straightened his elbows, but his mind was working badly.

"Now, now," is all he said.

The Repiev brothers went away looking worried.

Mishuka, boiling with rage, remained seated on the bench, the sweat pouring down his temples and nose from under his cap. . . . At last he brandished his fist in the air and struck the table such a blow that the boards split.

The brothers took the case of dueling pistols and came running back to the pond: the summerhouse was empty.

"Nalymov, Mishka, Mishuka," Sergei shouted.

The only answer came from a rook in its nest high up amid the dark branches.

"What do you think of that! He's run away," Sergei said. "I'll get him, anyway."

He loaded the pistols and fired twice into the air. . . . Echoes from all sides rolled across the pond. The sleepy rooks began screaming. Laughing, the brothers turned back to the house. They were met by Vera, who came out of a clump of acacias at a narrow part of the path. Her lips were trembling and her fingers were plucking at the fringe of the shawl on her breast.

"Forgive me, Nikita, Seryozha," she began, trying to stifle her gasps. . . .

"Good Lord, Verochka, what nonsense, go to bed," Sergei began; he saw her big round eyes full of tears and realized that something was going to happen which he did not want; lightly but firmly he pushed Vera aside, nodded to her, his eyes sparkling, and went away whistling.

Nikita remained with Vera. She slowly raised the shawl from her breast and covered the lower part of her face and her mouth.

"I suppose he has gone to wash," said Nikita, "he's covered with soot."

Vera looked up at the moon—her eyes were so sad and wonderful that, if Nikita had not been so shy, he would have asked permission to die at that very moment, so lovable were those eyes.

"Verochka. . . . Seryozha is very, very much in love with you," he faltered.

"All right, let's go home, Nikita dear."

Mishuka smashed his way through the bushes out of the thickest part of the garden, across the vegetable patches and

76

the flower beds; cursing and swearing, he stumbled over the ditches.

When the two shots rang out, he immediately sat down.

"An insult, a mortal insult," he muttered. "Help me, Holy Mother of God."

There were no more shots fired, no sound of a chase could be heard and Mishuka plucked up courage, began to curse again and, on his way, broke off the branches of the young apple trees. At last he got out of those devilish ditches and walked along a grassy glade beside the pond. A grey horse, its iron shackles rattling as it moved, was grazing beside the water.

"So that's who you belong to, you stinking creature!" said Mishuka, thrusting out his jaw. He ran over to the horse, twisted its tail and with all his might pushed it over the bank into the water.

The horse, snorting and baring its teeth, swam towards the reeds; Mishuka's heart became lighter, he began to think more clearly.

"I'll take their woods away from them," he said suddenly, rubbing his nose. "I've left them in peace long enough. They imagine the boundary runs along Chervivaya Gully: nonsense, it runs through the Orekhovy Hollow. There goes their Repiev Woods—phut!"

V

"We went to Moscow three times last year: we have a certain woman there, Sophia Ivanovna," said the Nalymov coachman, lying on the grass by the stables and chewing a straw. "She gets the young ladies for us. Some time ago she pushed Selipatra on to us—a skinny wench with a temper like the devil, but the master likes her. We brought her to the house and she immediately began kicking up a fuss: she started slinging all the other girls' stuff out of the window, their dresses and bags and things. The girls, Ha! Ha!, they ran out into the yard with nothing on but their shifts. And me and the master, we burst our sides laughing!"

77

"Your master's a godless Tartar, may the Lord forgive me," said a milkmaid who was sitting on the grass beside the gardener.

"That's because he's got nothing else to think about," put in the gardener. "When a man's got nothing to do, he always runs after the skirts. I once knew a man who lived with six women—and he was a decent chap, too."

The milkmaid sighed and adjusted her kerchief. The horses in the stables pawed the ground and crunched their hay.

The Nalymov coachman continued his story.

"On the last birthday, our guests drank for two whole days and those, who went out for the count, were taken to the ice-cellar to recover. And then guess what our master thought of—he took the guests up to the girls. The guests, of course, were excited and the master whispered to me, 'Go to the apiary and bring a tray full of bees.' I brought the tray and stuck it in the window. Everybody knows that bees don't like sinful goings on and they began to sting the guests on the bare parts of their bodies—and all the guests were naked. Me and the master, we burst our sides laughing."

The milkmaid spat.

"Yes," the gardener said. "But our masters are decent people and just and do not go in for such sinful goings on."

"They are just small people."

"And what if they are! And you, you slave, would be better to keep your mouth shut than to disgrace your master."

The Nalymov coachman was about to answer the gardener, but at that moment Mishuka approached the people on the grass.

"Harness up!" he shouted and turned his goggle-eyes on the gardener and the milkmaid. "What are you sitting there for, don't you see who is before you?"

The milkmaid got up. The gardener continued sitting where he was, rolled a cigarette and lit it, the flame of the match showing up his black beard.

"Didn't you hear me? Get up!" roared Mishuka.

78

"Go easy, master, you're not in your own yard."

Mishuka snorted and turned to the milkmaid.

"Who are you, woman?"

"A milkmaid, master."

"Here's three rubles for you, you fool! Cut off the cow's dugs. I'll give you another three rubles tomorrow. Understand?"

"What are you talking about, master, cut off the cow's dugs!"

"That's what I say, cut them off. Here's another half ruble for you."

"Take your money back, master. . . . What a sin, the Lord forgive me."

The horses were brought out. Mishuka climbed into the carriage, spat on the Repiev land and drove off; the air resounded to the melodious clamour of the Nalymov bells.

Everybody in the Repiev house had gone to bed, but there was still a light in Pyotr Leontievich's window.

Every night, before saying his prayers, Pyotr Leontievich went to his sister's room. At this time Olga Leontievna was either busy with the household accounts or was reading the leaf torn off the calendar for that day and wondering what meals she should order for the next day.

When Pyotr Leontievich kissed his sister's hand and gave her his hand to kiss, he always said the same thing:

"Don't forget to say your prayers, my dear."

This was what he did today. As Pyotr Leontievich kissed his sister's hand, he said: "Don't forget to say your prayers, my dear"; he went unhurriedly to his own room, closed the door softly and suddenly noticed a cockroach on the white stove.

Pyotr Leontievich pulled off his high boots and with a groan climbed up on to the shelf of the stove where he began saying a charm. The cockroach waved its antennae and fell.

"That's better," said Pyotr Leontievich.

Then he got down from the stove. It was at this moment

that the two shots resounded in the distance. Pyotr Leontievich opened his window and listened.

For a long time after the shots the garden was quiet; then voices, a man's and a woman's, could be heard.

"But, my dear, what can I do? I can't go on."

"Of course, of course, Verochka, you're right, you're quite right. . . ."

"Don't be angry with me, Nikita. . . ."

"I say again, you're quite right, there is no other answer you could give me."

"Good night, Nikita."

"Sleep well, Verochka."

The door on the balcony slammed to. For a time Pyotr Leontievich stood blinking in the darkened window. Through the walls he heard footsteps and the creaking of a bed. Vera had gone into her room and had begun to cry, at first softly but gradually louder and louder. She blew her nose. Pyotr Leontievich threw on a jacket and tapped at Vera's door.

"So you're crying," he said, sitting down in front of her and tapping his foot on the floor.

"Go away, uncle."

"Of course, I'll go away soon, but first tell me what you're crying about—does your head ache?"

"Yes, it does."

"Who fired the shots?"

"Seryozha."

"At whom?"

"At the rooks."

"Now, now, Verochka," Pyotr Leontievich said, placing his hand on her head, "my dear child."

"What, uncle?" Vera burst out crying still louder and buried her face in the pillow.

"Do you love Seryozha very much?"

"Yes."

"I'll fix all that up," said Pyotr Leontievich thoughtfully. "D'you know what—you go to sleep and I'll go back to my

80

room and think it out. In the morning, I'll go for a walk with you in the grove. We'll sit on the grass, you'll cry a bit, we'll talk things over and everything will be all right."

Pyotr Leontievich kissed Vera, went back to his room and stood in front of the icons where lamps and wax candles were burning; for a long time he could not gather his thoughts sufficiently to say his prayers, but stood smiling into his beard.

VI

Mishuka arrived at his house at dawn with the horse bells muffled; he left the horses at the stable and went up the back staircase to the girls' room in the attic with the idea that, if he came in quietly, he would catch the girls up to some mischief.

"Ho, ho, now I'll get them, now I'll get them," he thought, trying to work up a fury. The stairs creaked. He kicked open the door of the girls' room and looked around savagely.

All was quiet and sleepy in the stuffy room where a half a light came through the rose-colored curtains. Fimka and Bronka lifted their tousled heads from their pillows—they slept in one bed—saw their formidable master and immediately hid under the blanket.

"Get up!" shouted Mishuka.

Maria, smacking her lips and but half awake, stretched herself till all her joints cracked, yawned, looked at the master and clapped her hands to her mouth. Dunya turned over displaying her bare side. Cleopatra lay motionless on her back, covering her eyes with her sharp elbows.

"Vodka," said Mishuka to the sleepy-eyed Vanyushka who appeared in the door, "and something to eat. Get a move on!"

Going over to Cleopatra he said. "Rub the sleep out of your eyes, you old crow!"

He ordered the girls to stay in their shifts and not to dress. He took off his coat and seated himself on the sofa by the table, wheezing and looking round savagely until Vanyushka came in with a tray on which were delicacies of all kinds, a huge decanter of vodka and a round goblet belonging to Mishuka's great-grandfather.

Mishuka spread his elbows and set about his meal. He filled the goblet, shook pepper into it, drank it up slowly, frowning horribly all the while, and then stabbed his fork into a big pickled mushroom that took his fancy.

Maria opened her eyes wide and watched the pieces of fish, steak and ham, whole pickled cucumbers and patties smeared with caviare, as they found their way into Mishuka's mouth. Fimka and Bronka stood by the stove, shifting their weight from one foot to the other and slobbering at the mouth. Cleopatra sat with her legs crossed, her shift slipping down over her shoulders, and smoked swiftly and furiously. Dunya was adjusting her long hair. Mishuka suddenly choked on his food, snorted and burst out laughing, shaking the table with his fat belly.

Dunya immediately ran over to him, sat on his knee and began to pet him.

I felt so sleepy, but sleep left me when I saw you. What are you laughing at?"

"Toady!" Cleopatra snapped, blowing smoke through her nose.

"How that gelding . . . how I shoved that gelding into the water," Mishuka spluttered. "The gelding was their favorite, it's an old animal, they give it an easy time, and I shoved it into the water. . . ."

Fimka and Bronka puckered up their mouths, wiped them and smiled, as Mishuka got up from the table, stretched himself, still smiling. Dunya looked him ingratiatingly in the eyes.

"Will you lie in my bed?"

Mishuka did not answer, but went straight to Fimka and Bronka, seized them by their hair, and banged their heads together. The girls squawked and sat down. Then he went up to Maria and slapped her fat back. Maria gasped.

"Oh, good Lord!"

"Never mind," Mishuka said, "that's what I keep you for, you fat cow."

This was followed by tussles and horseplay. Mishuka was rolled over, roaring with laughter, by the crowd of girls that fell on him; he pulled them by their legs and their hair, rolled on the floor and gasped. The floor boards shook and the chandeliers rattled pitifully in the dimly lit drawing room below, a room that contained gilded mouse-eaten furniture, and the portraits of ladies and gentlemen in powdered wigs and was always kept locked.

Mishuka, tousled and perspiring, but comforted and happy, descended the inner staircase to his study where he lay down on the sofa and slept.

A heavy storm approached towards evening, the air was close and thundery. A fine warm rain fell straight down and rustled faintly on the leaves of the trees. Now and again a distant, bluish light lit up the windows.

Mishuka sat on the sofa with his hand under the sharp, pointed head of his favorite borzoi bitch, Snowball, and listened to the dreamy monotonous swishing of the rain that came through the open windows in the twilight.

Snowball turned her goggle-eyes on her master and again lowered her sleepy lids. At every clap of thunder she turned towards the window and growled. Mishuka stroked her head and thought about what had happened the evening before.

It was only now, sitting in the rainy twilight, that he realized that, the day before, he had been terribly insulted, that people had made fun of him, rejected him, had struck and frightened him, and even threatened to shoot him.

Mishuka growled when he realized all this to the full.

"They don't respect me, Nalymov. . . . They slap my face, me, Mikhal Mikhalych Nalymov—they insult me. . . . If I feel like it, I'll turn the whole region upside down. And they . . . me . . . Me—those . . ."

He pushed the dog off his knee. Snowball whined, crawled

under the sofa, and began to lick herself and snap at fleas with her teeth. Mishuka sat with his legs apart gazing at the indistinct patches of the portraits on the wall. Something had to be done: anger was gnawing at his heart. Mishuka began to think how he would tear off Vera's dress and horse-whip Seryozha—but these thoughts did not help him.

He rose heavily from the sofa and began to walk up and down the study. "Aha, you ignore me, well, all right, then. . . ." He picked up a paperweight and smashed it to the floor. "All right, ignore me." The hollow crash resounded through the empty house. Mishuka stood still and listened—everything was quiet. He took up an agricultural journal, which had been bound in one volume for five years—it weighed a good eighty pounds—and threw that on the floor as well. Another crash resounded through the house and then silence again—nobody responded.

"The scoundrels! They're not concerned about their master. . . . All they think of is thieving. All they want is to get money out of their master," Mishuka thought and suddenly remembered with disgust the recent tussle in the attic.

"Sluts!" he suddenly shouted out loud, "I'll show you whether you can sit on me! . . . Vanyushka!"

Mishuka crossed the dark room to the servants' quarters and shouted:

"Vanyushka, run to the stables and tell them that the master orders horses to be harnessed to two carts—and hurry. And send the steward to me. . . . Hurry, you son-of-a-bitch! . . ."

The rain poured in through the deliberately opened windows of the attic where the girls, tousled and disheveled, were sobbing as they tied up into bundles their dresses, underclothes and sundry cheap trinkets. Dunya was already downstairs sitting under a horse blanket in the cart, silent in her anger. Workers, soaking wet, passed by with lanterns, laughing at the girls. The rain splattered noisily in the tall poplars and formed big puddles. Maria, her face swollen from crying, came run-

84

ning from the porch, slipped and fell, her bundle flopping into a puddle: the workers roared, Maria whined and climbed into the cart. Inside the house Mishuka stood on the stairs leading to the attic, slapping his whip against his boot.

"Out of here, you filthy sluts," he shouted.

Fimka and Bronka, eyes wide open from fright, came tumbling down the stairs; Mishuka for a joke cracked his whip across their back-sides.

"Oh, Lord, they're killing us," Fimka and Bronka screamed as they splashed through the puddles to the carts.

They were put into the carts and covered with mats to keep the rain off.

"Kick her out, kick out the old crow," Mishuka shouted. The steward and Vanyushka finally dragged Cleopatra out. She fought them savagely all the time, bit their hands, twisted and turned, wild as a witch.

"You're fooling yourself," she said hoarsely to Mishuka, baring her teeth, "you can't kick me out, I won't go. I'm not your dog. . . ."

At last Cleopatra was put on the cart. The carts moved off. The workers, laughing loudly and waving their lanterns over the grass, went to their own quarters and were soon lost to sight behind a curtain of falling rain. Mishuka, finally satisfied with the outcome of the last two days and having taken vengeance for all insults given him, went into the house.

Not even the groom on the leading cart saw Cleopatra slip out of the second cart at a bend in the waterlogged road and hide behind the bushes in the garden.

VII

Pyotr Leontievich went into the boys' room, as it was still called from force of habit. Like all the rooms in the Repiev house it was high, had plastered walls and contained furniture that had suffered from the ravages of mice and moths. On the wall over the sofa hung the outspread wings of ducks, bustards, hawks and blackbirds, all of them thoroughly impregnated with dust. When anybody went into the room with a candle he got the impression of headless monsters crawling up the wall. The trophies belonged to Sergei, who never allowed anybody to touch them. When he had been presented with his first gun some twelve years before, he had used it from dawn till dusk shooting at everything in the garden, on the pond and in the fields until both the house and the garden had stunk so badly from the carrion that Olga Leontievna decided not to leave her bedroom.

As he glanced up, smiling, at the black wings on the wall, Pyotr Leontievich thought of the past. Those had been good times. So many nice people had been alive then. Seryozha and Nikita, both fine boys, were full of promise. Dear Mashenka had been alive then, always dressed in white, always kindly, always worried about how to feed her guests better, how to marry off one of her near relations or how to straighten out some unpleasantness.

Every day there was the noise of guests in the dining room or on the balcony; their uncle, old Nalymov, came often—he was a great joker and in order to astound everybody used to bite off a big piece of melon dipped in snuff. Olga used to come in from her excursions, beautiful, gay and mysterious, dressed in a velvet riding habit. She would strip off her long gloves and offer her hand to be kissed. . . . There were many, very many young men in love with Olga Leontievna in those days. . . .But everything had faded away like a mist, gone were the good old days. . . .

At that time Pyotr Leontievich had tried to set his sadly bedraggled affairs straight: he had built a cloth mill, but had not insured it, believing insurance to be the greatest of sins. A man should stand naked before his God like Job and should not take out insurance on his fortune. The mill burnt down. Pyotr Leontievich then thought of building a factory to preserve crayfish. There were untold numbers of them in

86

the Chermashnya River, they broke the nets and sometimes village boys, when bathing in the river, were nipped in the stomach and other parts of the body.

He build the crayfish factory and even ordered two majolica figures from Moscow to place at the entrance. Ten thousand jars with the factory mark on them were made, and it was intended to send jars of preserved crayfish direct to the big cities. The crayfish in the Chermashnya River, however, were suddenly stricken with the plague and died out completely. This was almost complete ruin.

Pyotr Leontievich then began to think of something more suited to this age of steam and electricity and built a horse-drawn flatiron for clearing snowbound roads.

Landlords and peasants came from miles around to see the huge flatiron forcing its way through snowdrifts amid clouds of steam and melting the snow with its hot sides. Six pair of horses dragged it for more than a mile. It was a frosty day and Pyotr Leontievich went flying down the road in a racing sled which upset, throwing him and dislocating his leg.

He ordered the iron to be placed in a shed and, since then, had not invented anything else for his estate. Solomino, and Trianon as well, went under the hammer and he was forced to send his boys into permanent residence with his sister at Repievka where he lived out his days in peace and quiet.

Engrossed entirely in his memories, Pyotr Leontievich stood twisting his snuffbox in his hands and did not notice Sergei enter the room.

"Did you want me, Papa?"

"Yes, I came to see you, young man. Close the door."

Sergei smiled, closed the door and stood before his father looking into his eyes with a faint smile on his face. Pyotr Leontievich took his son by the arm and screwed up his nose.

"Seryozha, tell me honestly, are you capable of loving anybody?"

"I am sure I am, Papa."

"You see, it's like this. Oh, Seryozha, if you only realized what a wonderful woman she is. You really are not worthy of her love. . . . You know, there's something in your eyes that is quite new to me, some sort of irresponsibility. . . ."

"You want to ask me whether I love Vera?" Sergei asked, derisively, almost angrily.

"Steady, steady, you're always running ahead. . . . I said there is an air of irresponsibility about you. . . . Vera is a wonderful girl, a treasure, a kind and beautiful soul. But it is dangerous to scare her. If you scare her, she will withdraw into herself for the rest of her life, d'you understand? . . . You have to be very considerate with her. I have become a matchmaker, you see, my boy. . . ."

Sergei walked up and down the room with his head bent. Pyotr Leontievich turned round and round towards him like a sunflower towards the sun and all the time blinked in a manner that showed he was growing more and more afraid. Sergei stood still in front of his father, did not look at him, but said firmly:

"I am sorry but I cannot marry Vera."

"You can't, Seryozha?"

"I greatly respect and love Vera. That's true. But still I can't marry her. What should we live on? Depend on Auntie Olga? Work as a clerk in the Zemstvo? Bring up a dozen children? I'm a beggar."

Pyotr Leontievich smiled pitifully and looked down at his own feet. Sergei again began to walk up and down.

"I am going to Africa," he said.

"So, so. . . ."

"To the Transvaal. In the first place nobody there has ever seen me before. In the second place there are diamonds and gold there. And Vera"—again he stood still and his black eyes flashed—"let Vera marry Nikita. That would be a good thing in every way. It would be honest, I think."

Vera sat toying with the piano keys. Olga Leontievna, her knitting on her lap, was looking out of the window at the creeping twilight. Nikita sat silent by the wall, his elbows resting on his knees. The birds in the garden had grown quiet. Vera kept striking the same note—middle E—softer and softer and then stopped and softly closed the lid of the piano.

"I'm going to St. Petersburg," she said after a pause. "I'll enter college, cut my hair short and wear an English fustian blouse."

"Stop it, Vera," said Olga Leontievna quietly.

"All right, I won't go anywhere, won't cut my hair and won't wear an English blouse."

Nikita got up cautiously from his chair, stood for a moment indistinct in the twilight and then left the room on tiptoe. Vera laid her head on the cold piano.

"Oh," sighed Olga Leontievna noisily, "how silly you all are."

"Does that include me, Auntie?"

"Judge for yourself."

"Auntie Olya," Vera said, without lifting her head, "am I very silly?"

"I think I'll go to my room and lock myself up, away from you all."

"I'm sorry for Nikita, Auntie Olya. . . . He is so . . . sad. I think I would do anything to make him get over it."

Olga Leontievna was immediately on her guard.

"Verochka, do you really mean that?"

Vera did not answer; her face could not be seen. Olga Leontievna went quietly over to her and stood behind her back.

"I know myself how hard it is to be jilted—that is something that even the most beautiful woman always has to fear —some men don't appreciate treasures, that's all." Olga Leontievna paused. "There is another treasure that you must never lose, Vera. Your soul must always be pure. Everything passes, love, happiness, insults, but the soul that is true to its own purity will come unscathed through all trials. . . . Your sufferings now are cleansing your soul." Olga Leontievna even raised a finger, her voice grew stronger. "Your tribulations have been sent you. . . ."

"Auntie Olya, I don't know what you are talking about, what tribulations?"

Olga Leontievna did not answer. She took Vera's head gently, pressed it to her and gave her a long kiss on her hair.

"D'you think that we old people have known so much happiness? Our youth was filled with sighs."

Vera sat up straight and slowly removed Olga Leontievna's hand from her shoulder.

"All right, I will stay with you always. I don't want to get married, that was only a joke."

"Oh, you're talking nonsense." In her despair Olga Leontievna even nudged her. "I don't want any sacrifices from you. I am not trying to send you to a convent."

"Then what do you want from me?"

Olga Leontievna seemed to grow smaller. Vera again bent her head. There was not a rustle in the house. If the wind had rustled the leaves in the garden, perhaps Vera would not have said what her aunt wanted her to say. There was just the same stillness of night in the garden, however, as though the whole world were holding its breath. Vera spoke in a whisper that was scarcely audible.

"All right. I'll marry Nikita."

Without speaking Olga Leontievna clapped her hands. She walked away on tiptoe, but outside the door her footsteps sounded light and merry—she seemed to be flying.

Nikita came in. He stood by the stove. Vera, still sitting in the same attitude, spoke without raising her head.

"D'you know?"

"Yes, I know, Vera."

"So that's that, Nikita."

90

She got up from the piano stool. She took Nikita's head between her hands and touched his forehead with her lips.

"Good night."

"Good night, Verochka."

"Bring me something to read."

"Would you like a new magazine?"

"Anything."

Nikita stood for a long time looking at the door, almost invisible in the twilight, behind which Vera's lightly rustling dress had disappeared. Then he sat on the piano stool and trembled in silence.

Vera lay on the low, chintz-covered sofa, an open book before her; she was not reading, however. A candle burned under a paper shade decorated with black manikins. Vera's eyebrows were drawn together, her dry eyes wide open. She kept raising herself on to one elbow and listening.

Several times already Sergei's voice had whispered, "Vera, Vera," from behind the bushes in the garden. She did not answer, did not turn to look, but she felt that he was standing at the window.

Then suddenly she jumped up. Sergei was standing outside the window, his arms on the sill. He looked at her with his flashing eyes and laughed.

"What do you want?" asked Vera, shaking her head. "Go away, go away from me."

Sergei jumped lightly on to the window sill and held out his hands. Vera looked at his short, strong fingers. He took her by the elbow and put his arms round her. Vera sat on the window sill, closed her eyes and did not speak. A deep shadow seemed to pass over her face.

"I love you, darling," said Sergei through his teeth. "Don't drive me away, don't be obstinate."

Vera sighed softly and lowered her head on to Sergei's shoulder. He bent over her but his lips brushed across her cheek.

"Don't, Seryozha, don't."

She could feel how fast his heart was beating. She could feel each heart-beat with her breast, with her own heart. Sergei seized her by the shoulders and began kissing her neck.

"May I come in, Vera, may I?"

"No." She threw back her head and looked him in the face, straight into his bloodshot eyes. "Don't touch me, Seryozha, I shall weaken."

He pressed his lips to hers. She could feel his fingers unfastening the hooks on her dress. Slowly and with difficulty she broke away from him. He fell with his head on her knees, his breath was hot. His fingers still continued unfastening the dress.

"Seryozha," she said, "leave me alone. I promised myself to Nikita today. I am his fiancée."

"Vera, Vera, that's very good . . . you know I can't marry you. . . . So much the better. . . . Marry him, marry him, it doesn't matter, you're still mine."

"Seryozha, what are you talking about?"

"Don't be silly, you don't love him and he won't be. . . ."

"What, what?"

"He won't know anything about it. Don't you understand he'll be happy with the very smallest of your kindnesses. . . . But I, Vera. . . . I'll go mad. . . . Everybody does it. . . ."

Sergei leaped into the room, blew out the candle and again took Vera tightly in his arms. She was like a block of stone. He whispered in her ear, sought her lips, but she struck him stubbornly and sharply in the chest with her elbow. Vera broke free from him.

"It's getting late," she said as she moved away from him. "I want to go to bed. Good night."

Sergei whispered a curse and then disappeared through the window. Vera did not light the candle; she lay down on the sofa again, her face in one pillow and another on her head, and cried as she had never cried in her life before.

IX

A seamstress appeared in the house: there were sounds of tearing calico, her sewing machine rattled and with her dry lips compressed, she held consultations with Olga Leontievna.

Nikita went to Simbirsk several times and visited the Chancery Council and the Bank of the Nobility. The house was redecorated, the carriage was reupholstered.

Vera lived quietly through all those days and rarely left her room. She sat at the window with a book and looked out at the blue water of the pond, at the yellow and green patches of wheat on the hillsides, and listened to the birds in the garden singing their songs of ancient sorrow.

Sergei went shooting every day, returning late with a full bag and smelling of forest, swamp and bird down. He smiled unpleasantly at Vera and, at supper, greedily ate a lot.

Pyotr Leontievich had grown more silent than ever and took snuff all the time.

One day Sergei went with his gun and his dog to the Nalymov woods, into the densest part where the ground was boggy. The pointer beat his tail against the ferns and from time to time turned, his intelligent, excited face to his master. Sergei caught his feet on fallen branches, stumbled through patches of open swamp, the dog's tail wagging, ahead of him all the time. Sergei kept thinking constantly, gloomily, about Vera.

How many tens of miles had he tramped in those last few days in order to soothe the pain, to quench that mad desire that was in him! Nothing helped him.

"Ph-r-r-r." A black grouse rose into the air. Sergei fired without even a glance. A few leaves fell from a tree. The pointer ran forward by leaps and bounds and sniffed about, wagging his ears among the ferns.

Almost immediately a horn sounded nearby. Branches cracked and a raucous voice roared through the trees.

"Who's that shooting in my wood! May your soul be damned! Who dares loiter in my wood?"

Sergei looked round him quickly. In a glade stood a huge,

ancient oak that was mentioned in all the chronicles of the Repiev and Nalymov families—hollow, rugged and with many branches like an heraldic tree.

At that same moment Mishuka, mounted on a roan mare, came bursting through the bushes on the other side of the glade. Waving his brass horn above his head, he shouted to his dogs.

"Get him, you sons-of-bitches, get him!"

Two pairs of Nalymov's red and white harriers, made straight for the pointer. The dog squealed and cringed at Sergei's feet: he seized it and thrust it into the hollow tree; then he jumped up and grabbed the lowest branch, pulled himself up and scrambled rapidly to the top of the tree.

"Get him, you sons-of-bitches, u-lu-lu," shouted Mishuka, his face flushed in anger. He rode up to the oak, circled round it, stood up in his stirrups, and slashed at the foliage with his whip. "Get down from my tree this minute. . . ."

"Uncle Misha, don't get so excited," Sergei chuckled climbing still higher. "you'll upset your digestion and that's bad for you." He threw down an acorn which hit Mishuka in the belly.

"I'll kill you! I'll whip you to death! Get down, I tell you! . . ." Mishuka roared.

"You'll never get at me, Uncle Misha, you'll get tired, waiting and you'll get hungry."

"I'll have the tree cut down."

"It's hundreds of years old, it's sacred."

"Get down, I order it, I, the elected marshal of the nobility in this district."

"I didn't vote for you, Uncle Misha, I never go to elections."

"Rebel! I'll order the gamekeepers to haul you down. I'll have you flogged."

The hounds leaped and jumped, howling in their fury. The pointer snarled, stuck his nose out of the hollow and snapped his teeth. Mishuka and Sergei cursed each other for a long time until the amusement began to pall. At last Sergei spoke in more peaceful tones.

94

"Why be angry with me, Uncle Misha? They've tricked me too. Vera is marrying Nikita."

"You are lying," said the astonished Mishuka.

"Instead of cursing each other, let's go to the farmstead together. We could have a drink there."

"Have you got anything to drink?"

"A couple of quarts of vodka."

"Hm," Mishuka said, "that's all very well. Still, you're a scoundrel."

"That's also true, Uncle Misha."

Apparently Mishuka was quite pleased with the idea of going to the farmstead for a drink after all the excitement. Sergei came a bit lower down the tree, winked at Mishuka and made a universally understood gesture.

"We can get that as well."

Mishuka threw back his head and roared with laughter, holding on to his saddle. Then he struck the mare with his whip and galloped away to the farmstead.

An hour later Mishuka and Sergei were sitting together in a warmly heated log cabin—Mishuka unbuttoned his coat and drank vodka by the tumblerful, perspired freely and made the table shake with his fat belly.

"Ha, ha . . . you're bold to come here, Seryozha."

"We have nothing to quarrel about, Uncle Misha, I like you. . . ."

"So you say. . . ."

"I like you, Uncle Misha, you have something of the old Russian titan about you, not like the gentry of today, scoundrels, small people. . . ."

"Small people, you call them, ha, ha, ha. . . ."

"You, Uncle Misha, are like one of the princes of olden times. . . . You have strength. . . ."

"A titan, you call me, a prince? Ha, ha, ha. . . .

"Let's go to Africa together, Uncle Misha. Oh, what couldn't we do there! . . ."

"To Africa? Ha, ha, ha. . . ."

"It's a pity I have no money, Uncle Misha, there I could manage something. . . ."

"You're a scoundrel, Seryozha. . . . I'll give you money and a good hiding as well, ha, ha. . . ."

A vigorous, husky young peasant woman, with a rosy face grey and twinkling eyes, came into the room. She sat boldly down beside Mishuka and nudged him with her elbow. Mishuka only grunted. Then the feasting began, and the timbers of the log cabin creaked and rattled.

X

Since early morning Olga Leontievna and Nikita had been touring the shops in Simbirsk, a carriage following them with their purchases. The horses were in a kind of stupor and the coachman had by some miraculous means succeeded in getting drunk without leaving his seat. Nikita mournfully dragged behind his aunt from shop to shop. He did not feel there was any need for all this fuss or for the things they had bought. He could buy up the whole of Simbirsk, he could dash himself against the stones and smash his head—Vera would not be the happier for it, her former vitality, the flash of her eyes and her merry laugh would not return: she did not love him, she did not love. . . .

"Come, come, young man, you look as miserable as a wet hen," Olga Leontievna told him, "a groom who cannot stay a moment without his bride. . . . All right, all right, we'll go home soon."

Auntie ran across the street to a shoemaker whose tousled head was bobbing up and down at his window—he was also drunk. . . . The horses and Nikita stood waiting despondently in the hot street. The coachman kept belching loudly; and every time he belched, he looked round scared.

"Oh, Lord," he muttered, "here's a fine to-do!"

By evening Olga Leontievna had finally calmed down; she climbed into the carriage, counted her purchases several times over and waved her hands to the coachman.

"To the ferry, Ivan. But don't forget to hold the horses on the hill, you're quite drunk."

"Good Lord," the coachman answered, "there's been no chance of a drink, I've been in front of your eyes all day long," and he belched so loudly that he could be heard all down the street; "what a fine to-do!"

They drove away downhill to the Volga ferry.

It was getting dark on the river and lights flashed out on the buoys and on the masts of the vessels. A paddle steamer splashed through the water in the distance. A mournful sunset was dying out over the low-lying farther bank of the Volga, over the trans-Volga region. On the bank the stalls loaded with cakes, the lemonade booths and stalls where women sold baked, salted and boiled comestibles, were lit up very cosily. The riverbank was redolent with the odors of hot bread, tar, hay and the river. The strains of a brass band came from the distant Venets Hill—the usual evening promenade had begun in the town gardens. They were playing a waltz or something like it that drifted sadly across the evening sky.

The ferry was just turning round an island and approaching the bank: it was a mass of heads, carts, sacks and bundles —for all the world like an anthill.

The fenders made of faggots on the sides of the vessel creaked, the office booth on the floating landing stage rocked, voices grew noisier, horseshoes clattered on the wooden decks —pushing and cursing, the drivers began getting their carts ashore.

A pair of spirited black horses, harnessed to a light phaeton, were squeezed between the sides of the wagons and were snorting in alarm. They trotted out on to the sand, the wheels whirring softly. Olga Leontievna ran swiftly towards the phaeton screaming wildly.

"Vera!"

The dark, closely-muffled, figure in the phaeton turned sharply round. The coachman pulled his horses up sharply.

97

"What's the matter with you? You don't look yourself! What's happened?" Olga Leontievna asked, pushing her way through the crowd towards Vera.

"Nothing has happened," Vera replied coldly in a trembling voice. "I did not come after you, I am going for a ride. Goodbye."

Silently Olga Leontievna seized the shaft horse by the bridle and turned the phaeton towards the ferry; she ordered Nikita to stay in his carriage and look after the parcels, while she herself got into the phaeton beside Vera.

"Where is the parasol?" she asked; taking it, she opened it for no reason whatever; she closed the parasol again and pushed it under the box. "Thank you, my dear, that was a nice trick to play on me."

Vera simply bowed her head lower and wrapped herself up to the eyes in her fluffy shawl.

XI

Three days before the wedding the large contingent of Repiev relatives arrived at Krasnov Hotel in Simbirsk.

Day and night boisterous shouts came from the rooms in which the half-dressed landowners played cards.

An unusual quantity of wine was drunk—and even more brandy. The empty bottles were stacked in heaps in the hotel rooms to astound all newcomers.

Frantic waiters were quite out of their minds as they ran along corridors hazy from tobacco smoke. Idlers thronged the square in front of the hotel, attracted by the noise and the lights.

"The trans-Volga landowners are on the rampage," they said to each other.

No lady would risk venturing into the part of the hotel reserved for men, on account of the cavalry attacks in the passages. Young soldiers—cornets, ensigns and gentlemen-ranker volunteers from the guards' regiments—dressed in their night clothes, sat astride chairs and dashed about the rooms on them waving their swords. Their commander was Mstislav Khodansky, a Pavlograd Hussar and Vera's cousin. The cavalry attacked passers-by in the passages, grabbed the women, and took the batteries of brandy bottles by storm.

The landowners, weary of sitting all night over the cards, went out in the mornings just as they were—deshabille—for a breath of fresh air in the town gardens where they upset the benches, wrestled wth one another, and shook the trees. The simple townspeople were horrified as they came to their windows still half asleep to watch these games.

On the fourth day the whole of Simbirsk was bathed in the fumes of wine and spirits. The police captain had to be taken to a pine forest across the Volga to recover. The landlord Okoyemov saw a devil looking out of the round vent of the stove. The idlers on the square swore to God that they had heard people neighing like horses in one of the hotel rooms.

At last the groom arrived followed by Olga Leontievna with her brother and the bride. Many buckets of ice-cold water were required to sober the drunken heads of the guests. At two o'clock the whole of the Repiev family gathered in the cathedral.

Sergei and Mstislav Khodansky held the crowns.* The bride was pale and sad, but indescribably beautiful. The groom kept anxiously putting his hand to his ear and asking the priest to repeat what he said. Olga Leontievna looked sternly at her relatives: some of them were standing glumly, staring at the flickering light of the candles, others had begun to crack jokes.

From the church, the young couple went straight to a steamer. Here the whole Repiev family drank champagne and hurled the glasses into the water. The steamer roared and cast off. Vera took out her handkerchief, waved to the people on shore and then put it to her eyes. Nikita smiled confusedly, and it was obviously that he did not understand or see anything.

The relatives went back to the hotel to feast. In the galleries at each end of the huge banqueting hall two orchestras played simultaneously. After the first toast to the "swallows that had flown away" Olga Leontievna wept. At that moment Mishuka walked importantly into the banqueting hall. He wore a long black coat buttoned up to the chin. His face was yellow and bloated and there were bags under his eyes.

He cast a dull glance over the long table. Everybody rose. Olga Leontievna's hands shook. Mishuka kissed her hand, and then went and kissed Pyotr Leontievich who did not even have time to wipe his mustache; he then sat down without looking at anybody and poured himself a huge glass of vodka. . . .

The orchestra in the galleries was about to play a polka, but Baldryasov, a government clerk on special duty who was acting as master of ceremonies, hushed them, glared with an air of suffering at the musicians and, standing on tiptoe, called for silence.

Mishuka ate half a pike, a fair portion of goose, frowned, and pushed his plate away.

"Although my niece insulted me," he began hoarsly and loudly, standing up to his full height, "although I said that I would not come to the wedding, I am here. I drink the bride's health. Hurrah! I shall not drink to the groom, he can drink for himself. And as for me, I'm going to die soon, so that's that."

He sat down heavily. . . . In a monotonous tenor Baldryasov shouted "Hurrah!" The musicians in the galleries began to play and created such a drunken uproar that even Mishuka looked up at them and muttered: "What canaille!"

The banquet lasted till dawn. At the request of the ladies the tables were removed and dancing began; cadets were invited from the local army school to provide partners. Card tables were set up. The young people crowded into the buffet. Miskhuka wandered amongst the guests, gloomy, heavy in his

100

movements and frowning disdainfully. Only once did he brighten up—on the occasion of a small incident after midnight.

In the smoke and crush near the buffet Sergei approached Mstislav Khodansky, took him by the braids of his hussar's jacket, and said to him in a drunken voice, swaying as he did so.

"Stiva, I think your cousin did a wise thing, eh?"

Mstislav Khodasky immediately threw up his head—he was a tall, muscular man with black curls and he was pale from wine.

"Stiva," Sergei said again, "Vera is a clever woman, you understand?" He shook his finger in front of Khodansky's nose. "She is smart and her body is hot and cunning."

"Go away and sleep," Khodansky replied.

"Stiva d'you realize that if I had beckoned her with my finger, she would have come running from the steamer. . . ."

Mstislav Khodansky's nostrils quivered. Just then Mishuka came up and pointed his hairy hand at Sergei.

"Spit in his ugly mug, he's a swine."

"I see that," Khodansky said, showing his white, even teeth.

Sergei smiled unhappily and pushed Khodansky. Mstislav Khodansky seized him by the middle and threw him on the plates on top of the sideboard. Broken glass was scattered on the floor. Mishuka roared with laughter.

"A fight, a fight," someone shouted as a crowd formed.

Somebody helped Sergei to get down from the sideboard. Baldryasov wiped him down carefully with a handkerchief. Sergei smiled crookedly and turned his flashing eyes on Khodansky.

"All right, you'll answer for this."

"Aha, a duel, that's good," Mishuka chuckled.

Soon after the seconds met in Mishuka's room at the hotel. They drank a lot of brandy and discussed the conditions for the forthcoming duel—a discussion that was full of nonsense and disagreement.

"Rubbish," Mishuka said, "let them fight in my room."

The seconds sat down and drank. Holding each other by the lapels of their tail coats, they went into conference.

"An eminently suitable place for a duel," they decided.

One of the seconds even uttered an unnatural shriek and slid under the table. A case of dueling pistols was brought and the principals were called.

Sergei came in, pale, and glared round the room. Mishuka pushed him over to the table.

"A drink of brandy before you die."

Mishuka himself loaded the pistols. The opponents were placed in opposite corners of the room. Mstislav stood with his jacket unbuttoned, his legs apart and his magnificent head held high. Sergei was hunched up, his neck drawn in as he looked around him with a piercing glance.

"Gentlemen," Mishuka said, holding the pistols high in front of him, "I hope that you do not want to make peace? No? You shouldn't anyway. Shoot from your places on the command one, two, three."

He offered the pistols, first to Mstislav Khodansky and, then, to Sergei. He went and stood in a corner, gasping, very satisfied with the whole affair.

Two candlesticks on the floor lit up the two opponents.

The seconds sat down and covered their ears; and one of them, holding his head in his hands, lay down on an ottoman.

"One, two," Mishuka began.

Just then the fourth second, a landowner by the name of Khrapovalov, a handsome man with black mutton-chop whiskers who was wearing high hunting boots with his dress suit, shouted out:

"Wait."

He took a piece of chalk from a card table, walked over to Khodansky and marked a cross on his chest; then went to Sergei and did the same to him.

"Now they may shoot."

Khrapovalov walked to the wall and stood there with arms folded.

"Three!" said Mishuka.

Two shots rang out together, filling the room with smoke. The second, who was lying on the ottoman, silently waved his legs in the air.

"They're alive!" Mishuka exclaimed in astonishment.

He took the chalk, turned Mstislav Khodansky round to face the wall, and chalked a cross on his back.

"Shoot at this."

Then he chalked a cross on the seam of Sergei's dress coat. The opponents began to take aim behind their backs. Mishuka began to command again.

"One, two. . . ."

Sergei staggered, said something unintelligible, and collapsed on the carpet.

"He's finished," Mishuka shouted. "It's God's judgment." Khodansky turned away from the wall and fired his pistol at a bottle of Veuve Cliquot. The grey smoke streamed towards Mishuka; he sneezed and moved his lips.

"Champagne. Horses. Let's visit the girls. . . . Pour some water over Seryozha and bring him to my carriage."

Early in the morning six troikas dashed through the peaceful streets of Simbirsk accompanied by whoops and whistling. The townsmen raised their heads and said to their sleepy wives:

"The trans-Volga on the rampage—Nalymov."

XII

Warmly heated stoves, a slight smell of well-washed floors, the winter light coming through frosted windows, acted soothingly on Olga Leontievna in her declining days. The time passed away quietly in writing letters, in conversations held in low tones and in the unhurried waiting for news.

The firewood spluttered in the tiled stove in a neat white room filled with soft light. Olga Leontievna sat at a little table near the window, writing a long letter in her tiny pointed handwriting. She turned over the crackling paper and wrote:

". . . I understand that constant melancholy—do your best to make sure, go to see a doctor. I think you must be expecting. God grant it is so.

"When the baby is born, see that you don't swaddle him: the English gave that up long ago, and I'll tell you a secret, this is already the second month I have been sewing little shirts and diapers. You are young, you laugh at your old aunt, but the aunt may still be useful. . . .

". . . You write that Nikita gets very tired at the office, sleeps badly and does not talk much. Don't worry, Verochka, that will pass. It's hard on him, but he's a good fellow. Go to the theatre more often, they say the Alexandrine Theatre is very interesting. Get to know some nice people, make friends. You mustn't sit there like owls on Vasily Island without ever seeing anybody and just listening to the howling wind—Pyotr Leontievich and I have enough of that here at Repievka. . . .

". . . Pyotr and I are getting on in years. One thing worries me—my brother has begun seeing some sort of light at night. In the mornings he wakes up in ecstasies. He still works as he always did, sawing and turning. He recently thought out a very useful invention—a machine to keep off mosquitoes in the form of a squeaker. You put this squeaker in the garden, it begins to squeak and all the mosquitoes sit around on the leaves, they cannot fly away and die of hunger. It's a pity we can't test it, it's winter now and there are no mosquitoes. You would die laughing. . . . And you, Verochka, be kind to Nikita, he loves you, loves you and will be faithful to the grave. . . . Eat the frozen chickens and the butter I sent you: I'll send another lot for Christmas."

The winter day came to an end. Cold, bluish shadows lay on the snow, the footprints in the snow became more sharply outlined. Olga Leontievna and Pyotr Leontievich sat at one end of the long table in the dining room drinking tea in silence.

104

The samovar sang in a tiny, soothing voice—it felt quite at home there. The big dining-room windows were half covered with frost.

"There was another letter from Seryozha today," Olga Leontievna said, "shall I read it?"

"Yes, please, Olenka."

Olga Leontievna read in a low voice.

"I returned to Cairo yesterday. I saw that old woman they call the sphinx and climbed the pyramids." (Pyotr Leontievich began tapping on the floor with his foot: Olga Leontievna looked up at him and he stopped tapping.) "A wonderful idea came into my head, auntie dear: I have decided to buy a mummy, cheap, at about fifteen rubles. I will cut out a piece somewhere from its back and hide it. Then I'll pack the mummy and send it to Russia. In our forest—you remember that place where they say there was once a hermitage—I'll bury my Pharaoh and sprinkle phosphorous over the top of him. Then I'll spread the rumour that, at the hermitage, a grave has been seen to glow at night. The people will come in crowds. I'll have to get some enterprising monks to go to that place and dig. They'll unearth holy relics. If you please, I am willing to sell the site with the graves and the holy relics together with the road leading to it. They will buy it and will build a hotel. They will send a telegram to the Emperor. Then I shall appear with my piece of the mummy: excuse me but this is my own Pharaoh, here is a piece from his back, and a receipt from the shop where I bought him. I'll get hundreds of thousands from the monks. There, you see, my dear aunt, the effect of an African sky—I am afraid I shall become a financial genius or shall marry a Negress. Simultaneously with this I am writing to Uncle Misha—my money is running short."

"That's not at all nice," Pyotr Leontievich said, after a pause. "It's not nice and he's restless. He was always an atheist and now he's blasphemous. Write and tell him not to write to us about Pharaohs any more."

105

One evening at twilight a messenger, one of the Nalymov workers, came to Repievka with a strange letter for Olga Leontievna. "Mikhal Mikhalovich is very ill and wants to see you," was scribbled on it in sprawling letters.

The Nalymov worker said that his master was really very sick and that the girl Cleopatra had written the letter: the master had not been able to drive her away from the house by any means, so he had got used to her and now she was looking after him.

Olga Leontievna got ready quickly and set out for Nalymovo in a covered sledge over the deep snow, across the dead plains lit up by a sad, icy moon surrounded by three bright haloes.

The sledge pulled up at Nalymov's porch at midnight. A faint light came from the dining-room window. The dogs bayed. A tall, gaunt woman in a black shawl came to meet Olga Leontievna in the outer room; she bowed low like a village woman. The growling of the white borzoi bitch came through the open doors.

"What's wrong with him? Is he bad?" Olga Leontievna asked as she removed her three fur coats. "And who are you? Are you Cleopatra? Take me to him."

Cleopatra went ahead, opening the doors and holding them open. The bitch whined in the darkness.

"In here, please," Cleopatra whispered at the door of the dining room. "He's waiting for you."

Olga Leontievna saw Mishuka sitting under a hanging lamp beside a round table covered with a stained and crumpled cloth. He was terrible to look at, swollen beyond all semblance to a human being. His bald skull was all scratched; his cheeks, yellow and swollen as if filled with butter, hid his eyes; and his snorting nostrils were scarcely visible.

Pieces of wood had been screwed on to the armchair under his elbows and to support his head; from these boards his arms and swollen hands hung down his huge body. He was breathing heavily and raspingly.

106

His green eyes, buried in his flabby cheeks, sought Olga Leontievna. In great fear she ran to him.

"Mishenka! What is the mater with you? What have you brought yourself to?"

"Cousin," Mishuka said with great difficulty, "I thank you." He began gasping for breath. "I have to sit all the time, I can't lie down. Dropsy."

"He's festering inside his chest," Cleopatra explained. "And he eats without stopping, faster than we can serve him."

There were, indeed, plates of food standing on the soiled tablecloth. Mishuka's bristling mustache and his treble chin were smeared with grease. Looking around, Olga Leontievna noticed a big jar of water on the table in which there was a white-bellied lizard with its legs outstretched.

" A crocodile," Mishuka muttered. "Seryozha sent it alive from Africa as a token of gratitude. It died today: that means that I too. . . ."

Olga Leontievna clapped her hands in horror.

"Have you called a doctor?"

"The doctor came today," Cleopatra answered, standing by the sideboard with her lips pressed together. "The doctor said that he would die today or, at the latest, tomorrow."

"T . . . t . . . t . . ." Mishuka muttered, with difficulty raising his drooping brows.

"What does he want to say?" Olga Leontievna asked. "To-morrow? Oh, it's hard for him to die. . . ."

"He's asking for the testament. . . ."

Cleopatra took a folded sheet of paper from the drawer of the sideboard and came over to the lamp.

That is why he sent for you, as a witness."

She began to read.

"All the ploughlands, meadows, forests and the uncultivated lands, the manor house, etc., I bequeath to Vera Repieva, née Khodansky, my niece three times removed, over the heads of nearer relations, in execution of which I have deposited bills to the value of a million and fifty thousand rubles at the Simbirsk court. I bequeath fifteen thousand in cash to the girl Maria Shitikova, nicknamed Cleopatra, for her loyalty to me and for the wrongs I did her. To closer relations, if such are to be found, I bequeath my blessing, but in lands and money—a fig."

With her lips pressed sternly together, Olga Leontievna listened to the reading of this strange will. When the reading was over and Mishuka, groaning and frowning made the sign of the fig—bequeathed to his closest relatives—with three fingers of uncommon size, Olga Leontievna burst out in alarm:

"Thank you, Mishenka, for not forgetting the orphan, but tell me, why do you do her this honor?"

"I wanted to dishonor her," Mishuka said. "Vera—that's why I made her that bequest."

"On account of her he drove us all out of the house, like dogs," Cleopatra said.

Olga Leontievna, thrusting her glasses and her handkerchief into her bag, stepped up to Mishuka full of determination.

"How dare you! The evil sinner—he wants to use his lands to exculpate his sins. One foot in the grave, shows us a fig and has mischief in mind. He'll remain himself and try to dishonor a woman on the other side of the grave. . . . Give me that will. . . ."

She grabbed the paper from Cleopatra's hands, screwed it up, and threw it in Mishuka's face.

"Farewell!"

Mishuka, glaring like a helpless dog, breathed rapidly, rolled his eyes and groaned. Cleopatra crawled under his chair after the crumpled will. Olga Leontievna had already reached the door at a jog trot, but turned and gasped.

"Good Lord, but he's dying!"

His face a deep red, his eyes protruding, Mishuka tried to get up. The boards that held him in the chair creaked and broke, the pieces fell to the floor. Suddenly the dog under the table howled wildly. Cleopatra, craning her sinewy neck and thrusting her nose forward, looked piercingly at the dying man.

108

Mishuka opened his mouth and stuck out his tongue as though he intended to swallow the girl in black.

"P . . . p . . . priest." The word seemed to be torn from his belly. He collapsed into the armchair, on the creaking springs. His head dropped forward on his chest. Blood streamed from his mouth.

Olga Leontievna made rapid, tiny signs of the cross.

"Lord, let thy servant depart in peace. . . ."

Cleopatra went slowly to Mishuka and covered his face with a clean napkin.

THE RAVINES

I

On a farmstead in the steppes, beyond the seven ravines, lived David Davidych Zavalishin, a landowner.

The deep ravines, which lay between his farmstead and the vilage, had filled with water to overflowing, and the roads over the crumpling, unstable ice, had all shifted; the low mounds bordering the ravines were laid bare; last year's shaggy burdocks still grew on them and the wind blew cold across the fields, rustling through the leafless willows.

Everybody was waiting, expecting, the water to burst through: men from the farm would run with lanterns during the night to see whether the dam had not given way; travelers had been languishing at the village inns for three days in succession, looking out of the windows at the already dangerous floods; the mail was not being delivered and local officials no longer went from place to place about their business. Only David Davidych was unconcerned.

He had lunched, drunk his tea, unfastened the belt round his silk blouse, and now lay on the sofa opposite the window.

The windows in the next room had been opened and he could hear a hen clucking in the sunshine; she was just starting another cluck when the rooster came up to her and she screeched in a voice that was not her own. Then a foal in the corral neighed loudly. The voices of the cook and the merry coachman came floating across the yard and, when they died down, the sleepy dog began beating its tail against the sides of its kennel. The sparrows jumped and chirped and fussed about as though they were drunk; the doves closed their eyes and cooed in honeyed tones; and David Davidych covered his ear with a cushion and tried to sleep. . . .

But it was hard for him to sleep—impossible, in fact; the sun on the well-scrubbed floor was hot, the new walls smelt of resin, a buzzing fly was whirling round in the shafts of light between window and floor; but the main thing was that everything that was happening in the room and outside belonged to its own world while he was alone in his. The fly alighted on his nose. David Davidych frowned, blew at it, grew angry, caught it deftly and held it, still buzzing in his fist.

"I'll feed you to the hen," Davd Davidych said, unwillingly climbing down from the sofa; he went into the next room, leaned out of the open window and called to the hen. At his beckoning, a white Brahma hen, his favorite, came strutting up; holding her head on one side, she looked at him with one red eye.

"Here, take this," David Davidych said, holding out the fly, but the hen pulled her head back suddenly and the insect flew away. It was quite warm in the sunshine and a scent of earth pervaded the air. Three paces away, however, there was still a crust of dirty snow; the farther one went from the house, the whiter the snow became; and David Davidych, raising his eyes, saw his fallow fields, still under snow, the mounds with their burdocks, the blue line of trees and, beyond it the modest white church with its bright cross.

David Davidych remained for a time leaning over the window sill, a frown on his forehead and the tips of his eyebrows drawn. His big, straight nose was slightly red; a light, curly beard and small mustaches covered his mouth, which was tight-pressed in a sorrowful grimace.

II

The three days preceding the flood, when all the forces of the earth were brought to bear on what was left of the recent supremacy of winter, when the earth shook itself in order to unfold, to give voice, to make itself heard—these three days had been a difficult time for David Davidych.

He was in his thirtieth year. That January he had separated

from his wife and had returned, after many years' absence, to the small family estate, where the garden had been cut down, the old house burnt and everything else that he remembered and loved, even what he could have lived on without any effort, seemed to have been uprooted or burnt.

The burnt-out house, in which Zavalishin had been born, had been so big and intricately built, that one was always discovering new rooms and nooks.

The garden, too, had been intricately designed, dark and mysterious; the apple trees, driven out of all other places by thick growths of acacia, bird cherry, lilac and black alders, flourished only around the balcony; beside the pond at the foot of the hill there was a constant clamor, day and night, in the century-old black poplars—in their hollows lived squirrels and owls, whole colonies of birds sang, hooted and whistled in the foliage and, at night, bats flitted about and toads croaked. Thick tall grass had grown up in the glades and in the long avenues of trees.

When David Davidych was no higher than his father's knee his mind was constantly filled with that riotously growing herbage. Tulips, wormwood, white and yellow clover, huge burdocks and timothy grass with dodder winding round them, waved and blossomed above his head: up above the undergrowth there were elusive moths and butterflies and evil insects that made loud noises. David Davidych lived in the herbage and grew up with it, he learnt many things from it—how to crawl unseen and attack, how to avoid attack, how to hide and how to run, bent low, in the green undergrowth.

When he grew older and wiser, the grass was just grass to him and nobody lived in it but beetles and hedgehogs. At that time he discovered a long, half-dark room furnished with black cupboards. Here were books, mice and the mouldy smell of wisdom. David Davidych would sit on a deep sofa and read adventure stories. He learned to love the carefree ways of animals and birds and all living creatures, but he began to regard the grass as something hostile and fought against it

112

with a wooden sword. He climbed the poplars, robbed birds' nests, shot arrows from a bow and killed tadpoles with a harpoon.

With each successive summer, however, David Davidych became more and more convinced that there was nothing extraordinary in the garden no matter how many dark corners he might discover and explore; he felt bored as though mysterious events lay ahead of him while the present was merely tiresome; there was nothing for him to do.

Later this expectation of the unusual and mysterious became a more frequent obsession with him and he thought life boring, frequently trite and familiar. In his boyhood, this expectation coincided with a domestic calamity. David Davidych's father often went away (at such times his mother was particularly sad) and, when he returned, went about looking depressed; David Davidych was sometimes awakened by his angry shouting, which came from the bedroom downstairs, and, on such occasions, he lay in his bed and wept. The next morning Mamma would be as pale and sad as usual; father, scarcely suppressing the wrathful glint in his black eyes, would run swiftly into the garden and distractedly stroke his head until it both bored and hurt David Davidych. Sometimes Mamma would run swiftly into the garden and press her son closely to her and kiss him as though he had been saved from some misfortune; but David Davidych did not understand this tenderness either.

One day his father came back from town accompanied by a small, dark-haired, perfumed lady, and Mamma suddenly became unusually vivacious—she laughed, rode on horseback, sang and went walking with the visitor. Soon afterwards David Davidych came upon his father in the garden—he was standing behind a big tree, his head sunk into his shoulders, a revolver in his hand; in the distance, Mamma in a white shawl was walking slowly down the avenue. David Davidych touched his father's elbow and he dropped the revolver, closed his eyes and let out a terrible scream. . . . That same night Mamma

113

awakened David Davidych, took him out into the back yard, seated him in a tarantass, and they drove on until dawn, when, on the fringe of the steppes, they could see the domes of churches, the water tower, and the houses of the provincial centre.

All that winter David Davidych, though bothered with grammar and theology, read Turgenev and then Gogol. In the spring he failed in all subjects, but at least he understood what mysterious encounters awaited him in the old house and garden.

During St. Thomas' week his father came to the hotel where they were living; he had grown very gaunt, but he was kind, talked with Mamma, and sat on the sofa covering his face with his hands; then he took his son back to the country. The small dark lady was no longer living there.

David Davidych, however, was not happy for long. The garden and the house cast new spells over him. He would penetrate into the dark undergrowth beyond the pond, look behind the big black poplars, move aside the shrubs of arbors where benches and one-legged tables were rotting away, go into the unused, dusty rooms upstairs, and look at the columns in the drawing room through the colored glass panes of the locked doors—everywhere he was afraid of meeting somebody; still he wandered about sadly awaiting this encounter. He had grown thinner and taller; dark rings formed under the eyes and he hid himself whenever he heard his father's voice; when asked whom he was longing for, he blushed; the garden became a fairyland to him, for *It* lived and hid there. *It* might turn out to be a girl, as in Turgenev, or a sun-tanned Ukrainian lass wearing a wreath of poppies, or a witch with bare legs, or even a mermaid.

Sitting on the trunk of a birch tree, which was bent horizontally over the water, David Davidych would gaze for long periods into the pond, at the water lilies, at the reflection of the reeds, at the calm, green water, and wait for a dangerous mermaid to rise out of the depths and, with graceful move-

114

ments of her arms, swim under the very roots of his birch tree.

One afternoon in June *It* did appear in the raspberry canes. "It" turned out to be a thin little girl in a blue blouse, barefooted and hatless, with a funny face and big eyes. David Davidych was disappointed when he saw that *It* looked so ridiculous, but nevertheless he went up to her, frowned and asked:

"What are you doing here?"

The girl smiled, looked at him, and ran away, tossing her plait of black hair.

David Davidych began to visit the raspberry patch every day and met her again, this time with a basket. He picked raspberries for her and they sat down on the grass; he asked her her name. The girl shook her head and lifted her blue eyes to the sky so that two clouds were immediately reflected in them.

"Perhaps you live in the pond?"

"No," the girl answered, "I live with Mummy, the priest's widow, and I'm called Olyenka."

When they had finished with the raspberries, David Davidych showed the girl over the whole garden and then took her to the library, where he began reading his favorite stories aloud to her.

At first the girl only laughed, but then she began to understand and listened with close attention; once she even cried bitterly over the touching description of a little girl who lost her way in the snow at night.

When David Davidych saw her tears, he immediately swore that he would never cause her such sorrow.

"Kiss the cross," said the girl and, unfastening a china button, she laid bare the brass cross on her meager chest. . . .

David Davidych kissed the cross and looked at the serious girl: she also looked at him, and then both of them blushed.

"Why have you gone all red like a coachman?" David Davidych asked.

The girl did not come any more after this; and to await

her coming he used to climb a tree from which he could watch the road overgrown with sorrel, the oak grove, and the church beyond it. He wrote his first verses sitting in that tree; they began like this:

> *A beggar, bent and blind and lame,*
> *With bag and staff walked down the lane,*
> *He met Dame Nature on his way,*
> *Lifted his bag and for alms did pray. . . .*

Quite unexpectedly his father returned from town accompanied by Mamma and they walked peacefully arm in arm along the avenues and sat on the balcony in the twilight. . . .

"Well, life did not turn out well, so we'll start all over again," Father repeated softly several times.

David Davidych was very pleased to have his mother back, and glad that he was no longer treated as though he had escaped some misfortune, but at night he began to be troubled with dreams that were full of tapping, rustling and running noises; and when he awoke, he heard the same noises and fell to wondering whether the old rat was not up to some mischief.

For a long time an old grey rat, as big as a cat, had been living in the house; it was so cunning and so evil that nobody had been able to kill or poison it. In the evenings it would climb on a chair and watch them eating, and when anybody went near it, it would whistle and jump high into the air; not long before it had bitten the drunken cook in the head.

Shortly after her arrival Mamma ordered a fire to be lit in a grate whose chimney had not been cleaned since the winter before and she and Father sat beside it in armchairs. . . .

Father looked at Mamma and his raised brows drew together; tears were falling from Mamma's eyelashes.

Suddenly the hot coals flew in all directions with a loud crackling and the rat, all covered with flames, leaped out of the fire and disappeared in a far corner.

Father ran about the house with the firetongs; Mamma seized hold of her son and did not calm down for a long time.

116

At last David Davidych was taken upstairs, undressed, and had the sign of the cross made over him many times; then he was told to go to sleep. He had scarcely closed his eyes before the burning rat ran into the room, described circles on the floor and began jumping higher and higher towards the ceiling. It suddenly reached the ceiling, ran round it in circles, crawled down the walls, squeaked pitifully, and began to shake the burning coals and flames from its body; the fire filled the room with a rosy light.

"Fire," came a voice at last, as though from a great distance. David Davidych sat up in bed and called his mother. The house was silent and dark. Somewhere, however, he could hear a creaking and crackling.

David Davidych pulled the bedclothes up to his chin and covered his head with a pillow but again came the penetrating, inhuman shriek of "Fire." This time David Davidych jumped out of bed and threw open the door. A bright red merry fire licked him with its sharpest tongues; the fire was raging on the spiral staircase as though it were a chimney.

David Davidych slammed the door and stood listening; soon, amid the general commotion he distinguished the voices of his mother and father: "David, David. . . ." He ran to the window, clutched the branch of a lime tree, and fell into the grass together with the broken twigs.

"Thank you, grass, I won't forget that," he said without knowing exactly why; he began to watch how the light flowed out of the windows—there were neither lamps nor candles in the rooms, but they were all lit up, and the curtains rustled as the tongues of flame played on the wallpaper. . . .

"That's the rat running about in there," David Davidych thought, and he ran across the damp grass until he reached the pond. A dense black smoke that seemed to be tinged with blood now rose from behind the tops of the tall trees that hid the house; then the smoke grew lighter and a fiery corona leaped and danced over the treetops.

"That's the King of the Rats climbing up," David Davidych

thought. . . . But the flames of the corona leaped higher and higher and merged into one huge flame that curled at the top, emitting showers of sparks. Shadows as black as pitch covered the grass as far as the pond; the water seemed alive and mobile, and the trunks of the birch trees glowed red down one side. The little birds folded their wings and fell from above into the fire.

Next morning the garden looked quite normal again except for the dirt on the bushes and on the grass. Carefully pushing aside the branches, Olyenka appeared nearby; she ran to David Davidych and took him by the hand.

"I told them you would be here," she said and she took him out of the garden to the back yard. Two figures covered with a curtain, lay on the grass beside the stables.

"Kneel down and pray for Papa and Mamma," Olyenka said.

David Davidych was taken care of by an aunt in St. Petersburg. He lay sick almost the whole winter, but by the spring he had grown taller, his voice broke, and it seemed that he had forgotten all about his father and mother, and about Olyenka and his vows. Then followed long years of schooling; with the aid of the generally-accepted methods these years produced a young man of the generally-accepted type who went out into the world to live his own life.

David Davidych had completed his training as a lawyer and began to look round for a place where he could settle down, but without coming to any decision, he set out for his native town; this at least was a place that he knew.

Here he noticed that most of the inhabitants lived without thinking or coming to any decisions, and enjoyed whatever pleasure came their way.

David Davidych was accepted as one of them, and he settled quite comfortably into the very lap of pleasure. He was appointed to the courts, he rented a flat, seduced the investigator's wife and began to think of himself as a nice pleasant young man and a menace to husbands. In the spring he took

118

a trip to Zavalishino. That once rich estate had been ruined by guardianship fees. A new wing stood beside the ashes of the old house; an ancient gelding, covered with lumps and bites wandered about the weed-grown yard, witness of bygone days; the farm buildings were empty and slowly falling to pieces, the garden had become thinner; vague and mysterious memories drove David Davidych hurriedly away without his even asking the steward for a report.

The following winter he was persuaded to marry Anna Ivanovna, a very rich woman of the merchant class. The gentry of the district had lost their lands and nobody was to be found to fill the post of Marshal of the Nobility. Anna Ivanovna had been educated in Paris, owned a mansion furnished in Empire style, and she wanted a coat of arms on her dowry. In general, there was no reason for not marrying her. Before the wedding David Davidych was advised to put his papers in order, and he made another trip to Zavalishino.

It was spring. Countless birds were singing and a rich odor came from the earth. When David Davidych, at some distance from the estate, saw the black poplars around his pond, he ordered the coachman to turn straight into the village without passing the homestead and to draw up at the church wall. The bricks of the whitewashed wall had been laid to make a pattern of pierced crosses. White lilacs in bloom behind the wall thrust their branches into the streets. As David Davidych entered the churchyard, he saw a girl in a white dress seated on a bench under a lilac tree and staring penetratingly at the newcomer. David Davidych bowed to her and asked where he could find the priest.

"The old priest has died," the girl said, rising and smoothing her dress. "The new priest is coming tomorrow, I am his fiancée. . . ."

'What a pity!" said David Davidych and explained that he had come to check his birth certificate, and gave his name.

"I know," the girl answered. "I recognized you, but you didn't—I'm Olga, the priest's widow's daughter. . . ."

119

"Impossible; excuse me, are you the same . . . remember. . . ."

"I remember," Olyenka answered, "but you had better go to the sacristan, he has the church books," and she went ahead of David Davidych, walking rapidly, but with a light and easy grace, straight into the church; while he looked through the books, she stood aside and waited.

He looked at her with a smile to which she did not respond and when, on the way out, he took her hand and said: "So we meet again, how strange. . . ." she pulled her fingers away and gave him such a look, her blue eyes darkening with indignation, that David Davidych did not continue the conversation.

He spent the night at an inn and next morning went back to the church to enquire from the deacon about Olyenka.

He learned that she had been educated at a Gymnasium and had remained in the village as a schoolmistress after the death of her mother. She had had many offers of marriage and even numbered the zemstvo doctor amongst her admirers; she had refused them all and it was only in the previous autumn (at the very time when David Davidych had paid his one-day visit to his estate) that she accepted the son of a priest, who was waiting for his ailing father to die in order to take holy orders himself.

Zavalishin left the church and walked down towards the river, where the ancient, dilapidated cottage that had belonged to the priest's widow nestled against an old willow. Olyenka was sitting at the window. She glanced up at him as he came towards the house and again there appeared in her eyes the same expression of what was apparently fear and indignation which he had seen the day before. David Davidych smiled and bowed; Olyenka's beauty aroused a strange emotion in him.

"What are you thinking about?" he asked, and again realized that he had said the wrong thing. He walked over to the window under which briar roses were in bloom and noticed that Olyenka was holding a little brass cross in her hand.

120

"I'm going to be married," Olyenka said and suddenly bent her head and frowned at David Davidych; he saw that her eyes were filled with tears; she tossed her head angrily and turned away from him.

"And I'm getting married too. See how everything has turned out," he answered; he felt a dull, hopeless ennui after he had said these words, and is seemed to him that everything was ancient history, useless and unfortunate. . . . "One has to live somehow," he added.

Olyenka did not answer at first, then she said hurriedly:

"Come away from the window, it will not do for the people to see. . . . So that's it, my friend."

She jumped up and stepped further into the room.

On the eve of the Fast of St. Peter, Zavalishin was married: Anna Ivanovna took him on a sea trip and then to Paris. On their return, he became Marshal of the Nobility, paid up the mortgage on his native Zavalishino, kept the most hospitable and luxurious house in town, owned race horses, and had a host of friends and, later, a mistress.

When he had tasted everything within the limits of his semi-somnambulant desires, David Davidych realized that Anna Ivanovna was a disgustingly bad-tempered and sensuous creature and that he himself was unhappy and unclean.

One night he came home in a bad mood. On going to his wife's apartments, he heard voices coming from the bedroom, her voice and that of a man: he pulled out his revolver and fired at the bedroom door; he did not even do it out of spite—the devil alone knew what for, just out of sheer cussedness.

Anna Ivanovna was offended and went to Berlin. David Davidych wrote her a brief but explicit letter on a piece of paper torn from a fashion journal and then settled down forever in his old home at Zavalishino.

III

It was not this story that David Davidych was pondering over as he lay on the window sill; nor was he thinking of effort fruitlessly wasted: he was still wrapt in a hazy, troubling expectation of *something* (an event or a catastrophe), something of tremendous importance; although his expectations had always deceived him till then, he still continued to believe that the present was the time for the most important thing to happen; as he rested, he was trying to get a glimpse inside himself, because he believed that, although the expected event would come from the outside, it would only gain full force and significance if it was confirmed within himself.

At that moment a young bay stallion, dragging with it the coachman who was holding on to the bridle, came dashing out of the stable with a clatter of hoofs. The animal halted in the center of the yard, swished its tail, neighed, reared, and then, together with the coachman, began trotting round the yard.

"A beauty!" David Davidych exclaimed, "What strength!" —and when the stallion's perky tail disappeared round the corner, he walked slowly away from the window with his hands folded behind his back. "The stallion neighs and rears, that means that spring has come; and nobody worries about the fact that the time will come when he will stop rearing, lie down and stiffen. Why should it not be all the same to me, of all people?" thought David Davidych, shuffling up and down his room. "Because the most important thing I am now expecting is my death; that's why."

He covered his eyes with his hand and imagined his funeral: it was a foolish scene, not a bit touching, even ordinary, and David Davidych pulled a face that was suitably sad and similar to those recently worn by people attending the funeral of the President of the Court. Then he imagined the death scene—himself dying in bed—and he shook his head: what the devil!

"No, no, it will be some other event, not death!" he decided hastily. "To get down to rock bottom, what makes me miserable? Everybody is the same, everybody has something wrong. I don't know a single happy family. Why should I be different from the others? . . ." He cracked his fingers and exclaimed in desperation: "But no, everybody probably believes in something or simply lives without thinking while I believe in only one thing—that I shall die and I don't want to. . . ."

At that moment the door was opened cautiously and a short, lean peasant appeared in the doorway: he was dressed in a shaggy sheepskin coat with a red knitted scarf wound several times round his skinny neck. He held his cap in his hand and blinked at David Davidych.

"What is wrong, eh?" he asked.

"I did not know you were here. . . . What d'you want?" Zavilishin asked, somewhat confused.

"I came to see you. Good afternoon," the peasant answered and held out his hand.

David Davidych took the hand and felt the hard nails and callouses. "He's not one to worry," he thought as he sat down at the table and pushed the tray with the vodka and sausage to one side with his elbow.

"Sit down. What have you come about? Who are you?" he asked.

"Andrei, Andrei's my name," the peasant answered, sitting down on the edge of a chair and casting a side glance at the vodka. "I had a hard job of it getting here—the water's running fast: the ravines will certainly overflow today. I don't know how I got here. . . ." Merry wrinkles appeared on his thin red face, he screwed up his eyes until they were tiny slits and shook his little beard as he said with deep implication: "We got wet through."

David Davidych poured out a tumblerful of vodka for the peasant and a small glass for himself. Andrei's face took on an air of respect; he took the glass as though afraid of crushing it and drank down the vodka to the last drop, gasping over-loudly to indicate that it was effective.

123

"Eat, help yourself," said David Davidych, pushing the tray towards him.

"Why waste the food," Andrei answered, "it only spoils the vodka. Anyway I don't see anything satisfying in that food. Give me milk porridge—you eat and eat until you're tired of it, then chuck down your spoon, to hell with it. . . ."

Zavalishin poured out another glass, and then a third, after which Andrei unwound his red scarf.

"We built a country cottage near Khvalynsk: the master was very pleased with it and gave us a feast, a real treat. We just ate and ate till we couldn't manage any more. Ivan Kosoy, he's a sawyer, an envious sort of a fellow, he said to me: 'Andrei, could you eat another pot of porridge for a bottle of vodka?' I said I could and ate it up. He was sorry to part with the bottle. 'Can you eat up that loaf for another bottle?' I said yes and ate the bread and he had to stand me another bottle. People began to laugh at me. But I was already getting into my stride. I went out into the garden and got watermelons, cantaloups and cucumbers, but all that raw stuff gave me a bellyache. . . . Such a bellyache that, when I eased myself, eight little chicks were drowned in my dung. It's a game, eating. But there's nothing to be gained by it."

"But I see I can drink a lot more than you," said David Davidych.

"Of course you can."

They sat quietly for a while, Zavalishin nodded his head, sighed with finality and then asked:

"But why did you come here, Andrei?"

"We're in trouble, David Davidych."

"Who's the we?"

"I've seen all along that you don't recognize me. And I can see your late Papa and Mamma as though they were still alive. I work for the priest's widow, I'm in service with her. . . ."

David Davidych's hand, lying on the table, trembled so much that he withdrew it and spoke without raising his eyes.

"What priest's widow? Olga Petrovna?"

"Yes. We call her the widow now. Her priest was drowned just a year ago. She ordered me to swim if I must, but somehow to get to David Davidych and give him a letter."

Andrei fumbled inside the breast of his coat and pulled out a warm, crumbled letter.

Zavalishin rose immediately, turned to the window and read it.

"I did not want to, and should not have done it, but I can't go on any longer. . . . Soon, perhaps even now, it will begin again. . . . My conscious moments are so short and so distraught. . . . I must hurry. . . . Come to me . . . perhaps you can help . . . in any case . . . I want to see you very badly. . . ."

"I don't understand," said David Davidych re-reading the poorly scribbled letter, "is she ill?"

"She is very ill," Andrei affirmed, "she flops down, faints when she falls, and she writhes howling on the floor. Today we thought she was finished altogether. I remembered how your Mamma used to give the peasants drops: I told the widow and she seemed to brighten up and grabbed a pencil. 'Take this,' she said, 'take the letter to him, and tell, anyway, tell him it doesn't matter.' I didn't understand very much of what she was talking about. . . . So please give me drops of some sort, David Davidych, I'll manage to get back by nightfall I suppose. . . ."

"Drops," David Davidych said. "No. . . ." and he did not finish.

Andrei also opened his mouth and turned to the window. While they had been talking, they had to hear a dull thudding sound that grew louder as twilight fell: it was as though the ancient forests had risen again in the steppes and the trees were rustling.

"The ice has broken," said Andrei. "That's too bad, I can't get back to the village now and I left the cattle out."

It was not the roar of the spring waters that David Davidych heard amongst the rising gamut of sounds, but the voices of all the dear departed, all the tiny sounds of the past years, and he thought he heard his own voice—and it all rose before him in one single instant which made the strange noise so loud, imperative and triumphant.

"Go and order them to harness the sled," he jerked out, "I'll go myself. But you hurry, run and tell them to make haste. . . ."

IV

The bay, harnessed to a carpet-upholstered sled, rolled its blue eyes and pawed the snowy ground. David Davidych, buttoning his fur-lined coat, hurried down from the porch, got into the sled and took the reins: Andrei immediately sat down beside him.

"Why are you here? Stay behind, I'll go alone," said Zavalishin.

"But I can't let you go alone," answered Andrei.

David Davidych slapped the bay with the reins and it immediately broke into a trot, throwing up the snow and mud against the front board of the sled.

"More to the right, master, across the unploughed ground," Andrei said seriously after they had passed the dam. "We must cross the ravine higher up."

By this time the sun had disappeared behind a violet-colored cloud that blotted out the sunset. Its edges were tinged with fluffy goldlike fleece, and the sun's rays spread out behind it. When the rays had lengthened, faded and finally become extinguished, the fringe of the cloud turned red and then a deep crimson. The sky above the setting sun was as limpid as water, and higher still where the blue heavens were opaque, the first cold star appeared, and then the number of stars kept increasing until the whole sky was dotted with them. The patches of earth where the snow had thawed lay dark on the level steppe; the snow, still bluish in color, crunched as the bay trotted easily and rhythmically over it.

"Listen, Andrei, is it true that she didn't love her husband?" David Davidych asked suddenly.

Andrei did not answer immediately; holding on to Zavalishin's waist belt, he kept looking left and right, apparently dissatisfied with the path they had chosen.

"Why should she love him—he was mean and disgusting," he said. "It made me sick to go into his church, only the old women went to him. When he was drowned, we made a bit of a to-do, of course, and she was sorry, after all it's no good when a man is drowned for nothing, but it's easier for her now. Only she keeps having fits; they say that's because he still doesn't give her any rest even now he's dead. . . . But drive more to the right. . . ."

David Davidych, however, could no longer reach the upper ends of the ravines. A faint light appeared over the horizon opposite to where the sun had set and the crescent of the new moon rose over the steppes. Zavalishin, encouraging the horse with his voice and slapping it with the reins, drove it straight towards the ravines. At last a dark strip appeared in the snow ahead of them. Andrei placed his hands on the reins.

"That's clay, on the far side; look how the snow has settled down on the bank. Go easy, master."

David Davidych pulled up; the stallion stamped its feet and puffed out its sides. Andrei ran on ahead.

"It's sunk a whole two feet," he called back, "I came this way today as easy as anything. But the sled won't get through now, we'll have to unharness the horse."

They unharnessed the horse, removed the collar and saddle and moved on. . . The near bank sloped down and, between the snow on the steppe and the ravine, there was a stretch of open ground covered with crushed grass from which the snow had melted. Slipping and sliding Andrei ran forward but soon got stuck.

"The ice doesn't hold," he shouted. "To hell with it, it's shallow here," and he soon scrambled up the far bank.

David Davidych was of heavier build and sank deeper; the stallion, which he was leading by the bridle, lunged forward, sinking up to his belly, tore himself loose, reached the far bank in a single bound, and stood still, shaking himself.

They could distinguish the belfry ahead of them and went straight towards it. On the humps between the ravines, lay oval pools of water amongst last year's stiffened grass. The moon was already high in the heavens causing the travelers and their horse to cast shadows; here and there the crescent was reflected in the pools.

There were seven ravines, and the middle one was the deepest and most dangerous. From the noise made by the water, one could tell even from a distance that it was in spate and was washing away the snow and clay.

Long before reaching the ravine, however, the two men were soaked up to the waist by the biting, icy water mixed with snow. At last they reached the middle ravine.

"I doubt if we'll get across," said Andrei. "It's bitter cold."

His beard trembled and the icicles hanging from it scratched against his sheepskin coat. He was wet through and did not know where to put his frozen fingers—he fumbled to get them into his ice-bound pockets or stuck them in his mouth. David Davidych looked at the belfry. It was now visible all the way to the churchyard wall, brightly lit up in the moonlight. It did not seem strange to him that the most important thing in his life at that moment was to get to the belfry as quickly as possible; he knew that it was dangerous and difficult but it was the right thing to do.

"Take the horse and go back to the farm, I intend to go on," he said softly.

Andrei groaned from the cold and answered as though he had not heard.

"If anything goes wrong, you hang on to the mane. It's a good horse and it'll get through; the main thing is to get to the clear water, you can se it near the other bank, look. . . ."

There, under the steep clay bank beyond the wide stretch

128

of patchy snow, he could see the ripples of the leaden water; the moon played on the running water and the ribs of ice. The ice in this ravine had broken before the others, and the water was pouring into the ponds on the far side of the village; the most dangerous place in the ravine was the strip of mixed mush ice and snow near the stretch of water. . . . There was no support to be found in the bitterly cold mush of snow and ice, there was no bottom, and you could neither swim nor crawl.

David Davidych tugged sharply at the bridle of the now docile stallion and walked along the yellow patches of snow. . . . Andrei strode along beside him, constantly reiterating:

"See you don't let go of the horse!" He ran forward on his toes and suddenly sank up to his waist. "There's no bottom!" he shouted and scrambled out, fell on his stomach, crawled a little farther, stood up and then went in again up to the chest not far from the stretch of water.

"It's all up," Andrei said; he spread out his arms and stopped moving—only his head and his cap stuck up from the snow.

"Hold on, oh please hold on, I'll be with you in a second, right now," David Davidych muttered, hardly able to speak; he let go of the bridle and began crawling towards the place where Andrei's head was sticking up. He spread his legs far apart, dropped his hands into the wet snow and shoveled it under himself from the sides; twisting and turning, pressing his feet well into the mush, he made his way forward. He no longer felt the cold; his face and his body inside the fur coat were burning; there was frost on his eyelashes which made it difficult for him to see; Andrei was already quite near; he turned his head towards the moonlight, rolled his eyes till only the whites were showing and kept opening and closing his mouth. . . . The snow had become quite liquid. David Davidych pushed his hands under his body and, groaning with pain, began to unfasten the buckle on his coat in order to free himself from this encumbrance. At that moment

129

the stallion neighed loudly behind him, reared and plunged several times.

"The bridle, the bridle," stuttered Andrei at last.

Zavalishin looked behind him. Apparently the stallion had caught his hoof in the reins, its head was pulled low down, its glittering eyes were bulging as it panted for breath.

"The bridle, loose the bridle," Andrei gasped.

David Davidych knew that he couldn't do it and that it did not matter—let the stallion perish—but all the same he straightened himself up, jerked forward and, crawling along, seized the bridle and pulled it free; the horse threw up its head, snorted and then kicked its hind legs in the air; its forefeet caught the skirt of David Davidych's open coat and, trying to grasp at something with his numb fingers, he stumbled under the snow of the icy water.

It may have taken him a minute or a fraction of a second to plunge into the greenish-black depths that choked his breath as they gave off that unforgettable smell of wet snow. Time, however, did not stand still for him. "The end," he thought. Then, "And thank God for that!" As he bade farewell to life, he saw calmly and clearly all his past days, saw himself as a boy, as a youth and as a man. All this appeared before his closed eyes simultaneously and in a strange perspective as though he, the onlooker, were not to one side or in the center, but on the periphery. He seemed to have become so large and boundless that he comprised within himself the earth, the sun, the stars, everything. . . . He realized quite calmly what was good and what was bad, when he had been foolish and when he had been wise, and he saw that he had been a fool to live without love like a blind man. And then, through this universe, rolled the stupid verses he had composed sitting on the tree. . . . This was followed by a bright even light, which darted swifter than lightning and burned up all the ghosts of his reminiscences— a living, exacting, joyful light. . . . David Davidych realized that he was alive and wanted to live. His heart was engaged

130

in a dull struggle. Water seeped into his mouth and his nostrils. He fought his way forward: the fur coat fell from his shoulders as though it were a pelt stripped from him and David Davidych, striking his feet against the icy bottom, rose to the surface, breathing hungrily in the stinging, piercing cold.

The stallion lay in front of him, its head and mane projecting above the snow; Andrei was hanging on to the mane. The horse and the peasant moved slowly out of the snow, and were whirled round into the clear water; the swift current caught them, spun them round and carried them away along the steep bank. A whole island of snow broke away behind them, opening the way for David Davidych who began to swim once he was clear of the mush; he, too, was carried away by the current and, for a long time, struggled to find a hold on the steep clay bank. At last he caught a bush where the bank was lower, pulled himself up on his chest, clear of the water, and then staggered away.

The clear, sharp-pointed crescent of the moon hung over his head. The whole sky with the stars and the moon was reflected in each oval pool; as David Davidych passed on, he crushed the mirrorlike surface of the puddles under his heavy boots. With the greatest difficulty he turned round to look back at the ravine. Andrei and the bay stallion were now close to the bank.

Exerting his last ounce of strength, David Davidych pulled off his boots and ran to the village. In the remaining ravines the water was only up to his waist. Beside the communal granary, on the brink of the last ravine, a grey-haired watchman sat motionless in the moonlight.

"Run and fetch help, there are people drowning!" Zavalishin said, pointing with his finger in the direction from which he had come; and when the watchman finally understood what he was talking about and hurried to the village, he continued on his way towards the white belfry behind which Olyenka's house stood between two lime trees.

V

Olyenka sat on a trunk covered with a felt mat, her head held between her thin hands. The blue linen frock she was wearing was badly crumpled; the black stocking on her left leg was hanging down and her shoe hung from her toes.

The candle on the card table between two shuttered windows was reflected in the dusty mirror; there were numerous tangled lines in the dust—apparently she had made them with her finger as she gazed into the mirror thinking of something else. It was a low room with plastered walls, the furniture was without any arrangement. A disheveled double bed stood against a windowless wall.

Olyenka closed her eyes and swayed back and forth from fatigue, afraid even to glance at the untidy bed. One of her attacks had just passed, an unbearable nightmare that had been tormenting her for a whole year. Olyenka was resting; there was not a single thought in her sick brain. Her tormented body, bent by the struggle, swayed back and forth like the pendulum that ticked alone in the silence, sliding back and forth between the flowers on the wallpaper. The ticking of the clock was the only sound in that room: even the cricket, the stove dweller, the merry companion of long evenings, was silent. A fly flew into the candle flame but at last it, too, burnt its wings, whirled round and fell.

Only once did Olyenka stop swaying and then she shuddered so that the shoe fell from her foot and the hands that held her head dropped to her knees. This, however, was involuntary, like belated lightning after a storm. . . .

A heavy fog wrapped her memory, her whole consciousness, and it was only the faint hope, like a spark in all this darkness, of an answer to her letter, the hope that she would again see the man whom she had always loved, that compelled her to continue her swaying movements, to cling to an unbearable life.

The steps leading to the hall creaked loudly, somebody entered and crashed to the floor. Olyenka turned slowly cold,

132

a pang of fear pierced her like a needle; she opened wide her huge eyes darkened by the ash-colored circles around them, leaped from the trunk, seized the candle and ran into the hall supporting herself by the jamb of the door.

David Davidych lay stretched on the floor, his arms bent under him. His jacket was frozen stiff and his heels in the torn stockings were covered with blood.

Olyenka put one hand to her throat and, holding the dancing candle in the other, screamed loudly. The cook, adjusting her kerchief, came sideways out of the kitchen door. Olyenka squatted beside the body and took David Davidych's head between her hands; she tried to lift it and look into his eyes.

"He came, he remembered," Olyenka said, turning to the cook. "He's breathing, he's breathing. . . ."

"Good Lord, I'll run for the neighbors, we can't lift him up alone," the cook cried and ran out into the street.

David Davidych began to groan and tried to get up by himself. Olyenka helped him, holding him by the shoulders. At last he managed to speak.

"Olyenka!"

"What, dear? What is it, darling? I can't manage alone, someone will come in a minute. . . ."

"Olyenka, thank God. . . ." he did not finish, but fell to the floor again, breathed deeply and then suddenly raised himself and sat against the wall.

His eyes were dim and his hair, stiff with ice, stuck out in all directions. He stared at the candle for a long time and then dropped his head on his chest. Olyenka sighed softly.

Three neighboring peasants, all brothers, came clumping in and bowed to Olyenka.

"You take his head, and you take his feet," they said to each other briskly, "don't knock him against the door." They lifted him easily, took him inside and sat him on the trunk. You must get his clothes off and pour two teacups of vodka with salt into him," the peasants said.

The cook hurried to fetch vodka and a cup, and David Davidych choked as he drank off the vodka; he sighed loudly, without opening his eyes, as though a heavy burden had been removed.

"The vodka's working!" the peasants said, and they had no sooner left the room than the cook ran back shouting.

"Where's the vodka? Oh, Lord, they're bringing our Andrei. . . ."

"Thank God for that," said David Davidych and collapsed.

With one hand Olyenka held him and with the other began to unbutton his wet clothes and pull them off, looking all the while at his face and smiling pityingly as he groaned. . . .

VI

David Davidych, covered with a blanket, lay in bed. His eyes were bright, his face red and dry. Olyenka went about the room quickly and with determination.

"You remember my oath," Zavalishin said, "well, I came. I'm quite all right. Only why do I feel so cold, Olyenka? It's as if I were lying on ice. I've been restless for days: I felt that something must happen. Surely it could not be death. I did not want to die! . . . No matter how I tried I could not guess what I had to do. There was the terrible minute when I sank under the water. It was really awful at first, but afterwards I felt all right. What a wonderful light I saw, Olyenka! It began out in the open spaces. And d'you know, I thought that the light was inside me."

Olyenka went over to him, stood quite close for a moment, and then began to pace the room again.

"I didn't understand your letter," he continued. "What did I have to save you from? Who was tormenting you? Your husband is dead. . . ."

"Be quiet, be quiet," Olyenka interrupted him quickly and then came and sat on the bed beside him.

He closed his eyes. She did not look into his face but past him, at the far end of the bed, as though there were somebody

134

by the wall. She stared for a long time and horror appeared in her darkening eyes. She slipped down to the floor, walked up and down for a while, and then sat down on the trunk.

"I know that it must be imagination or something," she muttered softly and despairingly, "but whatever it is, it's awful: he comes every night! Now he even comes during the day. He lies down, makes demands and threatens. And there is nothing but darkness here." Olyenka touched her head, "there are no longer any thoughts, only fragments. And I have no will power. I'm afraid, afraid. And now I have no strength left." She stopped, got down from the trunk and whispered: "He didn't die, I drove him to his death. I was never a wife to him. He used to beat me for it at night. He would kneel and kiss my feet and beg me till morning. Then he'd throw me on the floor. . . . All the time he spoke about you. Things went so far that he began to seek death and he held that over me as a threat. 'I married you out of spite,' I said, 'I don't love you, so how can I be a wife to you? Die if you can't bear it.' When they found him in the river and brought him home dead I knew that he would never leave me. Every day, every day, worse than when he was alive, he comes and torments me. He's here now. . . ."

David Davidych's cheeks burned. Raising his knees under the fur coat that lay on the bed, he exerted all his strength, breathed noisily, smiled and, freeing one hand, took hold of Olyenka's.

"Don't think," he said. "Go and lie down."

Olyenka flung her arms round his head and pressed him to her.

"But he's here all the time, look!" she exclaimed piteously.

David Davidych turned his head. There, near the wall beside him lay the unpleasant stranger; he was gaunt and dark with a long, ugly face. His body, in a narrow grey dress, was stretched out, the head was sharply turned, the bloated eyelids were screwed up and covered God alone knew what eyes. . . .

David Davidych smiled wryly.

"So that's him!" he said. "Come after us, have you? To take us away. . . . I've just seen something else. I have seen the light come to earth and rise again. I have seen the Source of Life. I don't want to go with you. I'd like to chase you, to kick you out! How loathsome!"

David Davidych wanted to raise his hand but could not. He closed his eyes. A wave of heat ran over his body to his head, reached his eyes and burned into them. . . . He spoke more frequently, more incoherently. Animals came floating out from behind the stranger, out of the wall, ran across the blanket, dropped on to the floor, leapt under the bed, lifted it up and rocked it.

"Why do they torment me so?" flashed through David Davidych's consciousness. . . . Grasping the sheet tightly he began to think furiously—why? The bristles on the animals under the bed pierced the mattress and began to stab him in the back. . . . "Of what am I guilty and before whom?" Again the question seared his mind like a flame. . . . He made desperate efforts to gather his wits together and then realized quite clearly that the stranger was pulling the blanket off his legs, attacking him and stuffing the blanket into his mouth.

Choking, David Davidych leaped from the bed and knocked the candle over. Waving his arms in the darkness he shouted loudly for Olyenka.

Her tender arms immediately encircled him, hid his face in her dress, pressed him close to her breast, and a distant but familiar voice said:

"Don't be afraid, darling, I'm here, I shan't go away."

"Olyenka, Olyenka," said David Davidych, "forgive me. . . . I realize how wrong I have been. . . . I love you and I'll try to deserve you. . . . We must never part, we must not die. Let them curse and torment us, but we'll sit together in each other's arms, sweetheart! You are the only one in the whole world for me. What a great love is ours! How bright the light is!"

136

VII

There was no more ice in the gullies; and the last cold that came at night with the ground frosts had melted away before the rising sun. The belated travelers had long since left for their destinations: the landowners and the tillers of the soil were busy with the spring planting; the local authorities drove about with a clamor of bells as had been their wont; the roads had dried out, the grass had grown several inches, and the invisible larks flew high up under the sun. It was already April when David Davidych finally regained consciousness and asked the time.

Olyenka never left his bedside; she had listened to his ravings and prayed that her dear beloved should not die; with each passing day she loved David Davidych more fondly and more profoundly. Her love replaced all her former sensations and nobody now stood between her and her love.

Once only, in the early evening, when David Davidych was sleeping, his wasted arms crossed on his chest, Olyenka stood by the window; low down in the blue sky floated a single, strange cloud. Across the street came Andrei leading a calf on a rope; a black-eyed girl with her hair cropped, a lump of black bread in her hand, was running along driving a black and a white sheep and a ram into the yard; the sheep were not afraid and would not go in, while the ram, horns down, was eyeing the bread; across the street a grey-haired old man sat dozing on a bench outside a cottage; two village women, leaning out of the windows of their respective cottages, were cursing each other—and nobody paid any attention to the strange cloud. It was floating directly towards the window. Olyenka brushed her hand across her eyes, but at that moment David Davidych stirred and groaned and she, shuddering as though she were breaking through a spider's web, ran to him and knelt by his side; loving him with her whole being, with every tiny drop of her blood, she asked in tender pity what hurt him, whether he did not feel easier. . . . David Davidych calmly opened his eyes, smiled for a long time and then asked:

"Sweetheart, what time is it?"

When he dozed off again, now evidently on the road to recovery, she returned to the window. The cloud had risen higher over the house—it was violet underneath with dense white and rosy whirls; it looked like a floating island with churches, domes and white trees.

"That is our land," thought Olyenka. "How wonderful, no memories of the past, no evil thoughts."

VIII

David Davidych, wearing a sailcloth dressing gown and a woolen shawl thrown over his shoulders, was sitting on a bench under one of the linden trees. On the bushes and on the old linden tree under the windows, pale green leaves had come out and the sky, seen through them, seemed more blue. . . . The street beyond the garden fence was quiet; the villagers had gone to work in the fields. His steward stood leaning against the gate that led into the yard. . . .

"All right, do whatever you think fit. I'm still weak, as you can see, but, in a week or so, I'll probably come over and see for myself. Run along, old man," David Davidych said to him.

The steward sighed respectfully and walked away, his boots clattering merrily along the street. David Davidych did not care whether he planted wheat or oats or anything at all. He was waiting anxiously for Olyenka's white dress to appear again from behind the bushes of the kitchen garden.

He did not recall the past, indeed, it would have been difficult for him to do so, for the power of spring that made the earth green again divided the past from the present with a wall of haze. . . . He merely felt that, since he had been on the other side of that hazy curtain, a ray of light had fallen and touched his heart and led him into the present day.

138

He saw Olyenka's dress through the bushes. David Davidych coughed. He could have called, but he thought it would be much nicer if she came to him with a serious mien, her eyes asking why he was coughing. . . .

Olyenka heard him, bent down to pass under the branches, and took a seat beside him on the bench. Her thin face was tinged by the gold of the sunshine; her blue eyes looked up at him, a braid of dark hair lay on her white dress, her hands were stained with soil. . . .

"What have you been doing?" he asked.

Her lips, tinged with a golden down, trembled; she smiled but did not answer, looking all the time more deeply into his eyes. David Davidych had had no time to get a good look at her, for she had come to him so quickly; and he had wanted to see how she walked, raised her arms, turned her head.

"I think I must have left my handkerchief lying about somewhere. . . . Fetch it, please. . . ."

Olyenka rose lightly to her feet and treading lightly along the path went to the house, the hem of her white dress fluttering in the breeze; she turned her head as she reached the door (he saw how lightly she walked and turned; now she would shoo away a fly—and surely enough she did).

"Darling," he thought, and called to her: "No, I made a mistake, Olyenka, here's the handkerchief; come and sit beside me, why are you digging in the garden all the time?"

"We transplanted the turnips," she said. She sat down beside him, sighed, bent forward slightly and placed her hand in his.

David Davidych took her hand, kissed it, and without looking at Olyenka, thought how much better and finer it would be if he were to tell her the ideas that had long been entertaining. "We are like people who have been through fire," ran his thoughts, "and now we are like the first man and woman in the world, lovers, pure and wise. But we want to live and live for a very long time. How can we manage so as to live and still remain our present selves?" It was hard to say all this and, naturally, Olyenka would have asked: "But why should we change?" And that was something he could not answer. Besides, his cleverly thought-out phrases did not sound so clever when Olyenka sat beside him on the bench.

"We must become man and wife," he thought, "that's what I must tell her," and, glancing at the demure Olyenka, he put one arm round her shoulder and, with the other hand, played with her earth-stained fingers.

"Olyenka, I love you so much," he said.

She nodded her head in confirmation and continued to sit there quietly.

"Just think of it," he continued, "all our strength will go into thinking of that one thing and if we become man and wife —what a wonderful life that would be—I would love you and love everything and then, I think, I should love the whole world. . . ."

Olyenka pushed a strand of hair back from her face, and her attentive, grave eyes showed that she had understood so well, that David Davidych stopped talking. She held his hand on her knee and what had been a scarcely perceptible blush began to deepen and spread over her whole face. She opened her mouth, sighed loudly and then said:

"What are you talking about? Love me as you will. In whatever way it must be. . . . I don't merely love, I just live for that love. . . ."

In the twilight they went into the house and, without lighting the lamps, continued telling each other there was nothing finer than love, that one could only love once, that they liked each other tremendously, and that the heavens opened to man only at the moment of death, although they said less about that than about anything else. . . .

In the morning Olyenka opened the window with a trembling hand and the room was filled with the scent of earth and grass, with the chirping of sparrows, with human voices

140

and distant footsteps. . . . The blue sky showed clean, warm and azure through the burgeoning bushes. "That's my own sky," she thought. "It is so transparent, it has covered the whole world," and turning round, she said tenderly:

"You've been sleeping long enough."

David Davidych opened his eyes, looked at the slender silhouette of the young woman by the window, and thought:

"Olyenka, the sky, spring, happiness—that's what I've always longed for."

ARKHIP

I

A spider, its shaggy legs widespread, dangled over the white tablecloth, green-winged midges fluttered lightly round the lamp shade, a gnat had burnt one of its long legs and was dragging it along the table. . . . The ivy on the balcony rustled, a sleepy bird hopped about in the bushes.

Alexandra Apollonovna Chembulatova was breaking up a biscuit, nodding her grey head with a black lace cap that looked like a fluttering bat.

"Volodya is guarding the garden," said Alexandra Apollonovna with a kindly glance at her companion, the young landlord, Sobakin, a neighbor of hers, "I gave him a pistol."

Sobakin smiled, puffing out his round, rosy cheeks.

"I assure you that Oska, the horse thief, does not exist. The priest's horses were stolen and the rumor immediately flew round the district—Oska, they say, has come, but Oska is merely a collective name; popular fantasy has endowed him with mysterious strength and skill."

The old lady shook her head.

"No, it's all true: he stole the horses in the evening and next morning he was seen three hundred versts away. . . ."

"Was he really seen?"

"That's just the point: they say he is unusually short in stature, bald, strong, and has a thick black beard down to his waist. . . ."

Sobakin smiled faintly and shrugged this shoulders.

"He has appeared twice in this district," continued the old lady, "and he raised such a scare that the local gentry chained up their horses and gave the stableboys loaded guns. . . . Still he managed. . . ."

"If he's known by sight, why isn't he arrested?"

142

"The peasants won't give him away. They're afraid he'd burn them up just as he burnt up your Khomyakovka, about three years before you came here."

"To tell you the truth, Alexandra Apollonovna, I'm beginning to be afraid."

"You have every reason to be worried: if I had a stallion like yours, I wouldn't sleep at night, I'd keep watch all the time. . . ."

"Yes, that Wizard is a miracle of a horse: you'll see, at Christmas, I'll enter him in the races."

"Yes, it's bad, bad: especially as your Arkhip. . . ."

"Arkhip's a gloomy fellow, but he's very reliable; he's as shaggy as a bear, has eyes like a wolf's, but he's trustworthy. . . ."

"Ho, ho. . . ." said the old lady.

A high-school boy climbed to the balcony from the garden, laid a pistol on the railing and said with a groan:

"Grandma, some tea, please."

"Be careful with that pistol, mind where you put it," Alexandra Apollonovna said anxiously.

"But it isn't loaded, Grandma."

"That doesn't matter." And Grandma got up with a rustle of her wide skirts and covered the pistol over with a table napkin.

"Well, Volodya, how are your robbers getting on?" asked Sobakin.

"All right," answered Volodya, stuffing cheesecake into his mouth.

"Have you killed anybody?"

"I think there's somebody standing behind the willows on the dam, but I'm scared of walking across the dam."

"It's damp near the pond at night," said Alexandra Apollonovna.

The boy screwed up his eyes slyly.

"I've got some powder, Grandma. . . ."

"Where did you get it? Give it to me this minute. . . .

143

Volodya, don't you dare run away. Sobakin, please, run after him and take the gunpowder away from him."

Smiling, Sobakin went into the garden and was soon dashing past the balcony, waving his arms, looking like a boy himself; Volodya, bending low, squealed but did not let himself be caught.

"Children, children," thought Alexandra Apollonovna and counted the chimes as the clock in the dining room struck eleven.

"Volodya, where are you?" she called. "Come in to bed, it's eleven o'clock."

Just then a horseman rode past the fence and pulled up at the porch.

"Is Master Sobakin there?" called a voice.

"Who's asking for him," responded Alexandra Apollonovna in dry, businesslike tones.

"His man, Mikhailo."

Panting, his arm round Volodya's shoulders, Sobakin came up on to the balcony.

"Who's asking for me? Is that you, Mikhailo? What's wrong?"

"A misfortune, sir," said the invisible man behind the fence. "They've stolen Wizard."

When Sobakin entered his yard on a lathering horse, after a mad gallop across the dark fields, he found the stable door wide open and a crowd of peasants waving their lanterns and creating a terrible hubbub.

"Have they really stolen Wizard?" shouted Sobakin.

"A bad business, we didn't keep our eyes skinned. . . ."

Sobakin ran into the stable. The bolt was torn off the box and there was a hole near the floor in the outside wall through which the thieves had apparently entered. . . .

"Where's Arkhip?" asked Sobakin.

"We tried to wake him, he's asleep, drunk."

Arkhip lay on a truss of hay, his pale face, framed in a mass of black hair, thrown back.

144

"He's alive all right, they didn't touch him, but he's very drunk," said the stablehands, trying to calm Sobakin.

"Pour water over the scoundrel."

They brought water in a stable bucket, lifted Arkhip's head and drenched it.

"Pour the whole bucket over him."

When his head, shirt and trousers were soaked Arkhip sat up and looked round him with bloodshot eyes.

"Eh?" he asked.

"Arkhip, where's Wizard?"

Arkhip got up, stooped down, looked at the bolt and the empty headstall, looked even through the hole in the wall and then answered just as calmly.

"They've stolen him, sir. I wasn't watchful enough. . . ."

"We went to bed," said the stablehands all together, "and Mikhailo, he said, 'I'll go and look at the horses,' and then he ran back shouting 'They've stolen him, stolen him'. . . ."

"Why the hell didn't you devils chase them?" said Sobakin menacingly.

The stablehands smiled politely.

"What sense is there in chasing them? It was *him*."

"Who's he?"

"Why, Oska."

"Nonsense, there is no Oska."

"Oh, yes there is, that's his work, sir, don't you doubt it."

"Nonsense," screamed Sobakin, "get mounted this minute. . . . After them! . . ."

The stablehands shifted from one foot to the other, but did not budge from the spot.

"Well?"

"No, we mustn't."

"How can we catch him. . . ."

"He's a good two hundred versts away by now."

Sobakin ran to the house and shouted back at them from there.

"Saddle a horse immediately. And you, Dmitry, come here

145

and take a letter for the police superintendent, and hurry up!"

. . . Next morning, when interrogated by the police superintendent, Arkhip answered that he had been drinking the day before and had heard nothing; he only remembered that somebody fell on his chest and twisted his arms, but whether there were two of them or only one, and what they looked like, he did not know.

There was nothing to be got out of gloomy, bandy-legged Arkhip and he was taken to the lock-up; the superintendent, drinking off a glass of vodka that had been brought to him on a plate, shook Sobakin firmly by the hand in farewell.

"Arkhip is the cause of all the trouble," he said. "We'll make him pay." Then he went away.

The sound of his carriage bells died away under the hill and Sobakin, whistling, went out on the balcony, down into the garden and strode along the avenue of linden trees.

"There'll be an investigation, and then a trial, but I'll see no more of Wizard than I can of my own ears. The devils, what a horse they've stolen, the devils."

Sobakin was so upset he wanted to go somewhere, do something.

"No, I'll get that horse back, I'll find him even if I have to get him from under the earth," he muttered and stood listening for a moment.

Close by, as though it had dived out of the acacias, Madame Chembulatova's carriage, the harness bells jangling, flashed past the bushes and pulled up at the house.

"I'm very grateful to you, Alexandra Apollonovna," said Sobakin, going to meet the old lady, "just think of it, they've stolen Wizard and left no trace behind them. . . ."

"I warned you, but you didn't believe me; it's just as I said," exclaimed the old lady triumphantly. "That Arkhip of yours is the cause of all the trouble, it was the same with my brother. . . ."

They walked down the avenue, their arms behind their backs.

146

"There's a horsefair in Uralsk at the moment," Alexandra Apollonovna said. "Go there as fast as you can, your Wizard is more likely to be there than anywhere else. . . ."

"Go to Uralsk?"

"Go on horseback, it's the quickest and easiest way under the circumstances; my brother also went on horseback, they stole Vadim."

"And what happened?"

"He found him, of course, found the peasant who had stolen Vadim; he was arrested and my brother got the stallion back."

"I'll go, Alexandra Apollonovna, with your blessing. . . ."

"God help you," she said and she kissed his forehead as he bent over her hand.

For a long time they continued walking up and down the avenue, Alexandra Apollonovna in her silk crinoline and Sobakin in his short-tailed tusser jacket; the old lady gave him detailed instructions where to go, how to care for his horse so that it could travel four hundred versts in four days, where to put up. . . .

"And be careful of the Cossacks, they're cunning. . . ."

II

The dark steppe was warm, the stars lit up the road and the greyish road itself deadened the clatter of the horse's hoofs; a corn crake screamed in a nearby pit—there must have been a farmhouse somewhere near in the steppe. . . .

The farmhouses, treeless and waterless, grew up like mushrooms on the level steppes, studded with man-made mounds, the age-old road of the nomad peoples. There was a smell of dampness and smoke. Sobakin stood up in his stirrups to look round, saw a light, turned off the road and pushed on straight across the grass. Hearing the hoofbeats of his hack, dogs began to bark, at first softly, then louder and in unison; a night watchman sounded the alarm and Sobakin saw the dark outlines of thatched barns and cowsheds, while under the very

147

nose of his horse, at the sides and behind him, the farmhouse dogs, hoarse with fury, leaped at him.

The watchman appeared, whistled to the dogs and wrapped himself closer in his big coat. . . .

"Good evening," said Sobakin, trying to get a look at the man's face in the darkness. "Whose farm is this?"

"Cossack Ivan Ivanovich Zavorykin's. . . ."

"Is it far to the village?"

The watchman did not answer immediately.

"A long way," he said softly and to one side as though he did not know what villages there could be, nothing but the steppes.

"Can I spend the night here? Ask the master, I suppose he hasn't gone to bed yet?"

"He's in bed," answered the watchman despondently, "been in bed a long time already."

"Then what am I to do?"

"I'll ask him, you wait here." And he went away.

A little later lights appeared in three windows, the watchman came back and took the horse by the bridle.

"You are asked to come in," he said.

Sobakin went through the outer room past trunks covered with rugs, into a living room that smelt of sage and wormwood—popular protection against fleas—and leather.

Saddles, bridles and horsewhips hung from the walls and in the corner there was a big, dark icon.

"Very inconvienient," thought Sobakin, "intruding in the middle of the night."

A tall, bony old man, Zavorykin, came out of a side room, stroking his beard. He wore a blue Cossack coat fastened with a narrow belt round the waist, and the collar of his cotton shirt was open.

Sobakin introduced himself.

"You are welcome," Zavorykin greeted him in a deep bass. "I'm always glad to have guests."

In the light of the lamp his face with its tightly stretched

148

yellow skin, long straight nose and dark eyes was like those that the schismatics drew on their icons.

"Sit down, please. Where are you riding to? To Uralsk. . .. So. . . ." Zavorykin said in his bass voice, nodding and passing his hand up and down over his face. "They have driven a lot of horses to the fair this year, not like past years."

A barefoot girl brought in a samovar, some food and vodka.

Sobakin was shy and did not know quite how to behave; he drank off the vodka and, perhaps on account of fatigue, it immediately went to his head; he told Zavorykin why he was going to Uralsk, told him the whole story from beginning to end.

"I'll get Wizard back wherever he is," he finished with some heat.

Zavorykin listened without raising his eyes, frowned, and, when Sobakin had finished, rapped on the table with his fingers and said:

"I would not advise your going there."

"Why?"

"They'll kill you."

"What d'you mean, kill me?"

"My advice to you is to go back home. You'll breed another stallion, it's not worth losing your life for the sake of an animal."

"You know it's not the stallion that I value so much, it's more a matter of principle."

"I understand. You're a young man, Mr. Sobakin, a fine young fellow, but you have not yet acquired wisdom. You have come to me, you don't know me, you tell me the whole story and, for all you know, I may have your stallion. Eh? I just put that to you as an example. After that I wouldn't allow myself to be disgraced. There are no written laws in our steppes and our wells are deep—throw a man down one, fill it in with earth and the man's gone. Don't get scared, it's only an example I'm giving you; there have been such cases, there

149

certainly have. In our steppes the Cossack is king over forty thousand dessiatins—he holds human lives in his hands, apart from all else."

Sobakin's head was reeling from the stuffiness and from Zavorykin's talk and it seemed to him that the Cossack's face was like that of the black, old icon, which looked down sternly and persistently from the corner . . . the same reddish mustache above thin lips, the same sunken cheeks and accusing eyes.

He seemed to see two pairs of those eyes gazing unflinchingly at him and those framed in the tarnished silver of the icon were the more terrifying.

"It must be their steppe God," thought Sobakin.

"It's strange for you to hear it, Mr. Sobakin, you people in the towns are different: you look after your bodies but you drag your souls in the dirt. But here everybody's spirit is as free as a bird. The soul is simple and there's nothing to soil it, the steppe is clean. God walks in the steppe. Here he will judge us for our sins. Our sins are many, but much will be forgiven us."

Sobakin got up from his seat.

"It's stuffy in here. . . ."

He was terrified and wanted to get away from the old man's eyes.

"Maria!" shouted Zavorykin to the barefoot girl. "Bring the gentleman some cold water and show him to his bed in the outer room."

The carpet-covered trunks in the outer room seemed to be floating in the air, and he thought he could still hear the voice saying "God walks here, God. . . ."

"Theirs is an awful God," thought Sobakin as he lay down on one of the trunks, "the god of the grasslands. . . ."

The next morning, in order not to offend the Cossack, he pretended to go home but when the thatched roofs of the farmstead and the long poles with the rams' horns had disappeared in the hazy distance, he turned southward on to a

150

broad highway, and the sun, the perfumed breeze and the merry jog of his horse, made him feel happier.

Herds of wild, Siberian horses stood in crude stocks in a strong corral built in a field of couch grass.

The horses rested their heavy jowls on each other's backs, brushed themselves constantly with their tails, closing their eyes against the sun.

On all sides stretched the yellow steppes, not a hill or a tree in them, and behind was the noisy fair with the iron chimneys of the bakehouse ovens all smoking.

There was a roan horse that could not stand the captivity, and he leaped over the corral fence and flew off neighing into the steppe, breasting the breeze, his mane flying.

The Bashkir horse boys in their long faded cloaks and flap-eared caps began shouting. Then they jumped on saddled horses and gave chase. The leader was waving a lasso. Two others raced to cut off the fugitive. . . .

Whichever way the horse looked, the Bashkirs with their big ear flaps, were after him; he turned right, then left, but the noose of the lasso slipped over his neck, his tail was twisted, he was lashed with a whip, and the Bashkirs dragged him back to the corral. . . . The roan grunted, whinnied and fell; the Bashkirs loosed the noose around his neck and put him in the stocks.

"Won't he run away again?" Sobakin asked one of the Bashkirs.

The Bashkir grinned, baring teeth that shone white against his wrinkled face.

"Nay, nay, he's wiser now, buy him, mister. . . ." he muttered.

"No, I don't need a horse like that, if you had a black half-blood, about sixteen hands. . . ."

Some Russian peasants, all in new shirts, came up to them. They leaned on the top rail of the stocks and listened, their colorless eyes expressing the calm of warmth and rest.

151

A half-blind little peasant in a torn sheepskin coat shoved himself in amongst them, blinking his canine eyes.

"Buying a horse, master? Will you take a look," he hurried off, but then turned back. . . .

"What sort of horse?"

"A grey."

"No, I don't want it, I want a black."

"You don't know how to sell a black," a stout, round-faced lad put in suddenly, "I'll sell a stallion, or have I sold it? Eh?" and he stared like a sheep, even opened his mouth.

The peasants laughed.

The lad hiccuped loudly and raising a calloused hand began to sing.

"When I was a boy and free. . . ."

"Drunk as an owl," laughed the peasants.

"Or worse."

Sobakin smiled; the lad, who was really drunk, thrust his chest forward and, waving his yellow fingernail under Sobakin's nose, said:

"What the devil, I wanted to sell it to you, but I've already sold it, a stallion, black, with white stockings. . . ."

"You're pretty tight," said Sobakin, "what's the holiday?"

The lad did not answer and his pale eyes turned bloodshot. . . . Sobakin shrank back.

"What do you mean holiday. . . ." said the lad, threateningly moving up to Sobakin.

The half-blind peasant butted in hurriedly.

"Don't be funny, lad, the master's interested, so you answer him and then go away," and he pulled the lad by the sleeve.

"Let go of me!" roared the lad and his whole sinewy body tensed to strike a blow; a hairy arm, coming from behind him and clutching him round the waist, dragged him out of the circle of peasants.

"Get along, get along, calm down," said a bald peasant, a funny short fellow whose black beard shone in the sun and whose eyes darted back and forth like two mice.

152

"Let me go," cried the lad and tried to break away, his arms waving, but his comrade dragged him farther away towards the carts.

"Who's that?" asked Sobakin, quickly. "That fellow there, the bald one?"

The peasants glanced at each other and some of them moved away, but an old man, his hempen shirt unbuttoned at his black neck, answered him.

"Who?—Oska," and screwed up his eyes.

Osip was soon taken. Sobakin with the police chased him to a tea shop and there called to him. Osip turned round and wriggled like a spider in the hands of the policmen who fell on him, but they soon got a rope round his shoulders and took him off to the lock-up.

A howling crowd ran after them. Many of them no doubt had an account to settle with Osip, but had been very much afraid of him; now, however, they hooted and cursed him, and there were some who capered in front, shouting "Now what're you going to do, you thief?" and struck him a blow.

The policemen held the crowd back with some difficulty, and a bold police sergeant with ginger mustaches, who had suddenly appeared, ordered the crowd to disperse.

The fair was in an uproar until evening. Osip sat behind iron bars in a dark log cabin and, at the interrogation, denied all knowledge of the stolen horses.

"I'm Osip, it's true, but I never stole any horses and you're making me suffer for nothing."

Sobakin decided to try and find out for himself where the horse was; he would try to frighten Osip and then promise to intercede in his favor; late that evening he went alone into the cell where Osip sat.

He went in and stood in the middle of the cell but could not see anything; he could only guess Osip's whereabouts by his breathing. Sobakin spoke briefly and, as he himself thought, persuasively.

"Osip, everybody knows that you have stolen horses, you have many crimes to answer for, so it is better to admit them and I will speak on your behalf."

Osip did not answer.

"You know, it's not the horse that I value so much as the fact that I brought him up myself, he's like a son to me."

"That's true," said Osip calmly.

"You seem to understand, so why do you want to cause me all this trouble?"

"Why should I cause you trouble?"

"You are causing me trouble. I rode four hundred versts, suffered a lot and then, on account of your stubbornness, I lose my horse. Osip, oh, Osip."

Touched by his own words Sobakin moved nearer to him.

"Don't come near me, master," said Osip dully.

Sobakin stopped short and began to shiver from a cold, ticklish feeling that ran over him.

"Osip?" he called softly, and after a pause again asked, "Osip, where are you?"

Something struck Sobakin painfully in the knees, the door was thrown open and Osip, his head held low like a bull's charged across the room, butted into a sleepy policeman who flopped down like a sack, and disappeared.

"Stop him, stop him!" A number of hurried, frantic voices called. The police bustled about in the darkness.

In the distance the cry spread like wildfire: "Stop thief. . . ."

The sergeant ran up, buttoning his tunic as he came.

"Who's escaped? . . ."

"Osip the horse thief," said Sobakin, "it was my fault. . . ."

The invisible fair was soon in an uproar, lanterns swung low over the ground, there were women's voices and the barking of dogs. Men ran around without knowing where or why, shouting: "He's untied a horse. . . . Who? . . . Whose? . . . Ask him who. . . . Got away on it. . . . Riding horses! Turn out the mounted men! . . ."

154

Mounted men appeared above the crowd as though they had been lifted up and, pushing the people aside, they raced for the town, the river, the steppes. . . .

Sobakin himself hastily saddled his horse and galloped past the carts, following the sound of hoofs and fading voices.

His horse's hoofs beat the ground sharply and rhythmically, the warm wind sang in his ears, the shouts of invisible men arose and died out again. . . . Somebody rode across his path shouting: "We'll catch him, he won't get away!"

Ahead of him the sound of the hoofbeats seemed to grow softer and the voices louder. . . .

Leaping over ditches and grunting, the hack galloped on until suddenly it pulled up short on the edge of a cliff, not far from the mounted police. Sobakin could hear voices.

"The river boys, turn back."

"We'll get across."

"Break your neck on the cliff. . . ."

Then, from a distance away to the right, came the shouts and hoofbeats again.

Sobakin turned his horse and chased after this second group of shouting horsemen.

"Have you caught him?" he asked.

The men laughed loudly in answer:

"A calf, master, we caught it, it's panting and scared to death, all in a sweat. . . ."

"Huh, what hunters you all are!"

"He got away, he's smart," answered the men respectfully. His horse was badly winded and Sobakin rode slowly away from the horsemen along the river.

A warm wind was blowing, carrying with it the fragrance of marsh flowers; from a distance a long drawn out animal scream was carried by the wind, then silence.

"What's that?" shouted Sobakin involuntarily, straining his ears to listen; the shriek was not repeated, but he felt a dull pain in his heart.

Sobakin was already asleep, dead tired from all that had happened, when somebody knocked at the door.

"Your Excellency," he said, "they've brought Oska."

Half-asleep, Sobakin jumped out of bed trying to understand what the man was saying. . . .

"They've brought Oska," repeated the policeman, in a strange voice. . . .

"I'll come straight away, wait a minute, but no, you may go. . . ."

As he walked out into the open, Sobakin realized that a misfortune had occurred. There was a strong sour smell in the local lock-up and on the floor beside the stove lay a body covered with a bast mat. . . .

A policeman, squatting beside the body, spoke in tones of pity.

"Our peasants have beaten him up, listen how he gasps. . . . Oh, it's terrible. . . ."

Sobakin threw back the matting. Osip lay on his side, his bare, grazed knees drawn up to his stomach, gasping for breath, his glassy eyes gazing through half-closed lids.

"What's wrong with him?" asked Sobakin with a slight shudder, afraid that he had guessed right. . . .

Osip's bare buttocks were smeared with mud and blood, and from them a piece of wood projected for several inches.

"What's that?" asked Sobakin in a high-pitched scream.

Osip threw his grey face still farther back and quickly licked his dry, cracked lips. . . .

One of his arms was broken and hung loosely; the other, all blue, gripped tightly at his buttocks.

Holding on to the wall Sobakin made his way to the outer room, nausea rose to his throat, everywhere he could smell that strong, sour odor which reminded him of a grouse that had been brought down with its intestines torn out by the shot. . . .

"That's how they give them the 'Turkish treatment,'" said

the police sergeant, rubbing his stiff whiskers. "Very unpleasant. . . . Osip admitted the theft, asked us to release your coachman, says he wasn't mixed up in the theft, and he told us where your horse was. . . ."

"I don't care about the horse, oh, why did I start all this?" said Sobakin.

"Why, it's not your fault, the peasants have been awaiting their chance for a long time. Believe me, even we were scared of Osip. . . . And your horse is in the steppe, the Cossack Zavorykin has him."

Old Zavorykin did not come out for a long time. Exhausted by the day's ride and the excitement of the previous day, Sobakin walked up and down the stuffy room; his ears were ringing and he felt sick from the dust that filled his throat and nose.

"I'll simply tell him the whole story and of course the old man will hand over the horse," muttered Sobakin.

The flyspotted lamp over the table stank terribly. . . .

"Oh, hell, I'll be gassed by that thing; why doesn't the old man come? And suppose he gets wild, he's self-willed enough; of course he was just boasting about the wells, but I'll have to approach the matter tactfully, slowly. Oh, hell, how that lamp stinks. . . ."

"Good evening, master," said Zavorykin suddenly in a loud bass—he was standing in the doorway beating the top of his boot with a whip—"Have you come for the horse?"

"No, I don't insist, I don't insist at all," simpered Sobakin. "You already know what a funny thing happened."

"A funny thing, but I don't know who's going to laugh," said Zavorykin.

Silently, never taking his eyes off him, he walked up to Sobakin and placed a heavy hand on his shoulder.

"You pup!" he shouted suddenly.

He raised the whip over his head.

"I'll not permit you," Sobakin tried to scream; there was

a sickly smell of dust and sourness, green circles swam before his eyes, his throat turned cold and he dropped full length, stretching out like a child on the cold floor. . . .

Sobakin regained consciousness lying in bed in the outer room and the first thing he saw was Zavorykin's profile, gaunt and clear-cut under knitted brows, bending over him. . . . Sobakin groaned and shifted away from him deeper into the bed.

The old man leaned over him.

"Come to. . . ." he whispered. "Turned out badly, the devil led me astray, thought you'd come to disgrace me, and you, I see, are as simple-minded as a little child. Master, forgive me, I'm proud. I got angry because I was mortally insulted, I could have killed you and nobody would have known. . . . And you, I see, are simple. . . ."

The old man shook his head and his dark eyes had a kindly look in them.

Sobakin held out his hand.

"I am not angry."

Zavorykin stroked his head.

"Christ looks down on us and is filled with joy. That's the way to live, but we don't live like that, no. . . ."

Zavorykin kept talking for a long time, hazily, sternly, earnestly. . . .

"All right, master, sleep. You can go home later in the day, tomorrow; by that time they'll have brought your stallion in from the grazing herd. God forbid that I should take money from you; and that hack of yours is tired, you can take mine, I don't ride him very often. . . ."

III

Alexandra Apollonovna was cutting the pages of a magazine; the drawing room fires had been lit for the first time that day and the broad backs of the old armchairs possessed all the allurement of autumn leisure. The room smelled of coffee.

The high-school boy was sitting on the window sill idly

158

dangling his legs. The miserable garden looked quite helpless in the endless rain.

"Tell us about your adventures," he insistently asked Sobakin.

"I've told you everything, what else. . . ."

"Volodya, don't bother Mr. Sobakin," said his grandmother sternly, looking over her glasses at Sobakin, who was sorting grains of wheat on a sheet of clean paper.

"Poor grain," said Sobakin. "What else can I tell you?"

"Something about that coachman whom they took away that time—he's awfully mysterious."

"Oh, Arkhip. . . ." smiled Sobakin, "a mystery indeed."

"But really, what has happened to him? Did they release him?" asked Alexandra Apollonovna.

"I think so. I went to town, tried to intercede but they told me they couldn't release him without a trial—I think it was held a few days ago. . . ."

"I never liked that Arkhip of yours, he's bad tempered and he has an evil eye. He comes over here and wanders round the stables peering at things and afterwards something always happens. . . ."

"Belyachok had malanders on the fetlocks, remember, Grandma?" the boy put in.

"Yes, Belyachok had malanders; no, no I don't like people like that, you should have let him stay in prison. I'm not sure he's innocent," the old lady took off her glasses. "Before you came to the village, he beat up my watchman just because he would not allow him to drive his cart through the wheat —just imagine, he deliberately drove his cart through the wheat. . . ."

"I remember," said the boy, "how they brought the watchman here, it was ghastly: his head was dangling and flies were crawling over his face."

"Strange," drawled Sobakin, "Arkhip has never been quarrelsome, always obedient, quiet. . . . Although there was one strange incident. . . . D'you remember last year I drove away

159

from here in the evening, that was when Father Ivan had been impersonating a turkey; I don't know why but, instead of going the usual way, we drove straight across the pasturelands and behind the boundary post there's a deep ditch; I said to Arkhip that the night was dark and that he should remember the drop on the left. But he just urged the horses on. 'Steady, Arkhip,' I said. I knew that we were right on top of the ditch but he did not seem to be able to hold the horses. . . .'"

"Horrible," shuddered Chembulatova, "and what next?"

"The horses themselves turned suddenly. 'What are you doing?' I shouted, and he turned round and said in a dull voice, 'God saved us, master, God kept us out of danger!'"

"So there you are, I told you so, tomorrow I'll order them to fence off that place. . . ."

"All the same I think that was just an accident; what have I or my horses done to him? And he could have killed himself too."

"Landless peasants like Arkhip, who have no families, are capable of anything, they have the devil in them. He works for you and everything seems all right—he's moody and silent, and then suddenly he goes and sets fire to your house. . . ."

"Grandma, look, the weather's clearing up," shouted Volodya and before his grandmother had time to say a word he threw open the balcony door and a fresh breeze, carrying with it the scents of damp earth and leaves, burst into the room, rustled the leaves of her book, and splashed raindrops on it; the sun, peeping out through breaks in the clouds cast its rays on the raindrops, the windowpanes and the yellow foliage. . . .

The door was closed and there was a clatter of crockery in the dining room.

"Never mind about the Arkhips," said Alexandra Apollonovna, sailing into the dining room. "You only get upset, and the cause of it all is that the peasants are not properly looked after. The peasant reverts to his primitive savage state. . . ."

Sobakin recalled a newspaper story that he had read a month before in a St. Petersburg left-wing newspaper that

160

accidentally came his way, but he didn't want to think about it; it was warmer and cosier as it was.

Towards evening the wind died down, the low sun tinged the leaden clouds hanging close to the earth a deep red and, spreading its pale wings far over the wet yellow steppe as though in farewell, sank behind the horizon.

The burdocks on the dark mounds were still clearly visible, and the puddles on the shiny surface of the road turned a dull violet.

The rattling wheels splashed fresh mud into his face, spattering his hands and the reins.

Sobakin unfastened his leather coat and sat bouncing up and down on the seat, wrapt in thought.

"Here they are, these expanses of steppeland, untraveled roads, forgotten burial mounds. There is no end to them and the villages are just as grey and forgotten; the people in them are like grass, untalkative; God alone knows what they live for, from one generation to another, without change, like wild rye."

Boredom, the sister of the autumn wind, went from road to road, from mound to mound, over the ploughlands and through the villages singing doleful songs. . . .

The iron tires of the wheels rattled on the road as the horse's hoofs beat the ground and slipped as they went downhill. . . .

The gig rolled and jolted into a ditch, the horse slipped and fell on its knees.

"It's hard for an unshod horse to pull up the slope," thought Sobakin and slapped the animal with his reins. . . .

Behind him he could hear frequent short steps as though someone were trying to overtake him in silence. . . .

Sobakin turned his head: a peasant dimly visible in the darkness of the hollow, was running after him waving his left hand.

"Strange," thought Sobakin and still not understanding

161

what was quite obvious, he lashed the horse smartly with the whip.

The man was overtaking him: it was easier to run on the grass, it was not so slippery.

"The devil alone knows what sort of a chase this is, what does he want?" Sobakin thought and rising from his seat he lashed the horse with the whip. The horse leaped into its collar, slipped, reared up on its hinds and dragged the gig up on to level ground.

"Hi!" shouted the peasant sharply and suddenly started back.

"Arkhip! Is it you?"

"Hi!" shouted Arkhip again, stopped short in his run, raised his hand and threw a bright gleaming axe, his body bent forward, waiting. . . . The axe struck the bottom board of the box heavily and fell at Sobakin's feet.

"What's the matter with you? Have you gone out of your mind? . . ." Sobakin shouted, pulling in his horse. Arkhip followed along behind.

"Now you can do what you like with me," Arkhip said, watching the crimson strip of sunset—grown greyer now and all wind-blown.

"What are you trying to kill me for, Arkhip? I haven't done anything, Arkhip. . . ."

"You killed my son."

"What son?"

"Osip. . . ."

The strip of sunset turned darker, grew narrower, and closed its crimson eyelid.

Sobakin moved on at a walk. Arkhip walked to one side a little behind him.

"Arkhip, I'll say nothing about this to anybody, but swear that it will never happen again. Listen, Arkhip. The peasants killed Osip, I would never have allowed it."

Arkhip laughed softly, like a wild horse neighing, and Sobakin saw his white teeth for the first time.

IV

Over a year passed. The new summer, scorching the earth, had clothed it with a coat of gold, the grain had been harvested and the barns smelled of fresh straw; every day the threshing machine rattled away until sundown; at dawn there was a ground frost that fled at the first sight of the sun; and only in the dark garden and on the meadow where the shadow of the house fell, the tiny sorrel leaves gleamed silver.

In the morning the peasants again came to Sobakin to lodge a complaint against Arkhip.

All the summer Arkhip had given them no rest; he drove their cattle into the master's cowshed when they grazed it on the master's land, when a laborer cut grass for himself from the master's field he would take it away, besides grabbing the culprit's cap—come and complain, he would say, and bring the fine with you.

And as to the grain—not a sheaf of it did they see until the last kopek was paid into the office. Arkhip had become such a zealous steward that one wondered where all his viciousness had come from.

The peasants wanted to beat him up, but he either evaded them or put the blame on the master—said it was not his doing but the master's. The peasants kept their wrath secret and in the autumn, when the master's fields produced ten bushels of grain for every three produced in the peasants' own fields, they decided, each by himself, to set fire to the master's barn.

That was the tradition handed down by the old men.

In addition to this the "golden charter" had come to the vilage—nobody had read it, nobody had seen it, but then everybody knew what was written in it; the document was an old one, it had been traveling the earth for a long time.

After the charter came leaflets; they were read and the people were seething with excitement in a dull sort of way, like an underground spring.

"Well, Arkhip, and how are the peasants?" asked Sobakin, yawning, as he gave his instructions for the next day.

Arkhip shrugged his shoulders.

"How are they, fools. . . ."

"This morning they came again to complain about you, you can't keep on like this, Arkhip, you'll spoil my relations with the people."

"You can't handle the peasant any other way—press him hard and he'll do whatever you like for you; but if you say a good word to him, he'll hang on your neck."

"I've heard they're going to burn me up."

"Who knows?"

"They set fire to Chembulatova's barns."

"That's just mischief, the lady went away to town and they got into mischief."

"All right, you may go Arkhip. And see to it that the horses are harnessed in the morning."

"Are you going somewhere?"

"To town."

Arkhip went away and Sobakin got into bed; before going to sleep he opened a catalogue of flower and vegetable seeds, but soon the flowers all began to look like ladies and then all of them like one and the same lady with an upturned nose; a head of cabbage, shaking itself, put on glasses and turned into old Chembulatova.

Sobakin, half-asleep and smiling, thought how good it was that he, so strong and young, would again soon see those flashing eyes, that little snub nose and that golden hair. . . .

Sobakin was awakened by a loud whisper.

"Master, master, get up."

Sobakin jumped up, his bare feet on the floor and, without understanding anything, looked up at the excited Arkhip who was standing in front of him, a candle in his hand.

"What's the matter?"

"The peasants are coming."

"What peasants, where?"

164

'They're coming here, to you. When I ran here, they were already crossing the dam. . . ."

Sobakin listened and looked helplessly at the strong, moody Arkhip.

"Arkhip, what can we do?"

"I've bolted all the doors, master, and you get a gun. We'll have to scare them off."

"There are no shutters on the windows."

With trembling fingers Sobakin rammed cartridges into shotguns, which he pulled down from the wall above the bed.

"I'll load 'em with ball, then they won't try it again. . . ."

"Good Lord, what an idea!"

The hum of voices and cries became more audible in the darkness outside, they could even hear individual shouts; suddenly there was silence and the waiting became unbearable. . . .

"What are they doing?" whispered Sobakin.

A windowpane smashed with a loud ring and a stone, falling on the writing desk, overturned a vase of feather grass; cries resounded through the broken windowpane.

"Smash the windows, let him come out."

"Hi, master, come out, we want to talk to you."

"Give us Arkhip. . . ."

Arkhip, nimble and agile, jumped over to the wall, brushed his thick hair out of his eyes and said imperatively:

"Put the light out, master. . . ."

Sobakin blew the candle out and it was all the more unbearably terrifying as the peasants shouted still more ferociously.

"Come out. . . ."

With a rattle several more windowpanes flew out and Arkhip screamed savagely. . . .

Pressing close to his sweaty back Sobakin whispered to him.

"What's going to happen? My God!"

"If you don't come out, we'll fetch you," shouted the peasants and several heads in fur caps appeared at the windows.

165

"Get in, boys, there's nothing to look at. . . ."

Arkhip fired. . . . Everything immediately became silent. . . . Under the window somebody was groaning, frequently and penetratingly.

The peasants stood back from the house, talked matters over, and their disputes became louder and louder.

"Fetch some hay, some straw," shouted several voices.

"Burn him up."

"Smoke the swine out."

"Catch him! Catch him!" came excited shouts.

There was a whine, a trampling of feet and dull blows.

"They're beating up our workers," whispered Arkhip. "Now there's nothing left for us to do but to run into the garden, they're going to set fire to the house. . . ."

"The balcony doors are sealed tight."

Arkhip did not answer but lifted his gun and fired. The shot lit up the walls, the overturned armchair and Sobakin in his nightshirt, without his trousers. . . .

Arkhip fired again without aiming and the acrid smoke filled the room. Sobakin also fired and the gun recoiled and struck him in the shoulder and cheek.

Suddenly a red flame burst out under the window and crackled loudly.

As the light increased, the peasants ran off with shouts of joy and a stone struck Sobakin in the face. . . . The wound bled and Sobakin clenched his teeth and groaned. Arkhip, pressing Sobakin down to the floor, crawled out into the corridor. A bright light coming through the open doors filled the corridor. . . .

"Now, master," said Arkhip, "I've been wanting to thank you for a long time. . . ." Pushing Sobakin down he sat on his chest and laughed.

"Arkhip, what are you doing, Arkhip?" whispered Sobakin, trying to get free; he tore Arkhip's shirt, scratched his body but Arkhip became like one drunk, fury filling his whole body.

166

Pressing his knee into Sobakin's throat, he pulled out a jackknife with a bone handle, opened it with his teeth and looking straight into Sobakin's white insane eyes, he drove the knife in.

The house was burning. The peasants, lit up by the flames, stood with serious faces watching the fire devour the dry walls and creep out, smoking, from under the eaves. . . . Roselit Pigeons circled round. . . .

"Look, there's Arkhip in the stables," somebody shouted.

Dragging Wizard by the bridle, Arkhip came out and, when the shouting peasants ran towards him, he threw himself flat across the horse's back and, pressing close down on his withers, drove him off across the steppe, all lit up in the glow of the fire. . . .

And that was the last that was seen of him. . . .

THE MAN IN PINCE-NEZ

Early in the spring, two of the cottages of a small resort straggling along the shore of the sea were taken possession of almost simultaneously.

At the wooden house with a tower (known in those parts as "The Castle") drew up a cart loaded with huge baskets. A thin, morose man with a blond beard, wearing a raincoat and a wide-brimmed hat pulled low over his eyes, got out and climbed the porch steps where he stood waiting for someone to open the door. He frowned and adjusted his pince-nez as he glanced at the cold sea and the shreds of cloud skimming the grey waters. The wind inflated his raincoat and caused the bare branches of the poplars to wail like whips.

Then he entered the damp, unheated cottage, glanced at a couple of pictures showing rocks and boats and at an old calendar gone yellow on the 23rd of August and, without taking off his hat, sank down on an ottoman which emitted a cloud of dust.

Presently he said, "Make a fire."

The keeper, a Tartar who had just dumped the last basketful of books in the dining room, answered "All right," and went away. The man remained alone. Drawing one leg up under him, he lighted a cigarette and sat gazing at the bare trees blowing in the wind beyond the dusty window. The sea was out of sight, but its dull roar filled the house. Twilight descended. The cigarette between his listless fingers went out, and the man gave a cold, muffled yawn that made his teeth chatter.

Some three hours earlier, the neighboring one-storeyed cottage had been taken over by a young woman accompanied by a nurse and two little girls in blue sheepskin jackets. For three hours the cottage was all hustle and bustle. Now the lights were burning, the children's beds were made, and some milk was being boiled in the dining room. To the warm nursery came an old brown dog which extended its paw and gave a one-sided smile to show its unselfish devotion to the new arrivals. The young woman, her head and shoulders wrapped up in an Orenburg shawl, had taken a seat on a little porch sheltered from the wind. Between two pillars she caught a glimpse of the sea far down below, and it was as novel, strange, and expressive as the theater. The woman was sure that tomorrow, and for many, many days thereafter, she would watch that sea, sometimes in bad weather and sometimes in warm, when all the surroundings would glow with life and color and the waters would be transformed from lead-grey to azure.

The gentleman, who had just arrived, was named Nikolai Ivanovich Stabesov. He was a Moscow bachelor with a sizeable income, and had taught an elective course at the University. The revolution of 1905; a brief exile; then the anxious, shameless, dissipated ten years when, in the intoxication of luxury and sin, the world was preparing its explosion of hate, and finally the war itself, had completely undermined the health of Nikolai Ivanovich. He had suddenly felt utterly alone, lost, and unwanted. As though a sturdy army boot reeking of dubbin pitch were poised threateningly above his head, Nikolai Ivanovich could no longer sleep, work or see his friends, and so the doctors had sent him to the Crimea.

The woman in the neighboring cottage, Yekaterina Vasilievna Bolotova, had come to the Crimea for the sake of her younger daughter, whom the doctors found to be suffering from rickets. Madame Bolotova feared and disliked doctors, but she had brought her children to the Crimea notwithstanding, and all along the way had meditated happily upon this latest change in her life. Her husband had died several years before. A certain sadness lingered after this loss, but life did not seem barren and hopeless. Her husband had never roused in her an impassioned love, and the separation had caused her

169

no great sorrow. Besides which she had youth, her children, a little money, a little freedom, and the happy faculty of always dreaming about the beautiful and the unknown, about the sea, the green fields, the warmth of summer when the bees hum and the earth is lavish. . . .

These two people who had become neighbors on this lonely seashore were destined to meet. And it would hardly be expected that their meeting in such an isolated spot would make as little impression as the passing of two people on the streets of that great city where it seems Stabesov and Yekaterina Vasilievna had once made each other's acqantance and had spoken to each other (though when and about what, neither of them had the faintest recollection).

A gravel path ending in a flight of steps led from the porch straight down to the sea. Here Nikolai Ivanovich would sit facing the sea with a book, with his hat and pince-nez pulled down on his nose. When the wind became more boisterous and the waves, breaking against the rocks of the shore, showered the high embankment with sea spray, he would move up the steps. And the stronger the wind blew, the louder and more alarming the echo from the rocks resounded, the higher the spray flew, the more definite became the mood of Nikolai Ivanovich—a mood which he expressed in words muttered through clenched teeth: "Go ahead and blow, my dear. You and I are both 'natural phenomena.'"

Then chilled to the bone, Nikolai Ivanovich would go home, throw himself on the divan, light a cigarette, take up a book, glance at the title, read the concluding lines of the last page, mutter something like "Hm, so you're sure of it? I envy you all right, I certainly envy you," and toss it on the window sill. Reading had become revolting to him, like stuffing an empty stomach with cotton. "High time to be publishing your own book," he would say, going to the window and drumming on the glass with his fingers. And both his "own book" and the pose at the window were loathsome to him. "What rot," thought Nikolai Ivanovich.

170

Only at night, as he lay in his damp bed with his skinny legs drawn up under him (thinking to himself—nobody but me needs such legs, not a soul in the world), did Stabesov experience his only honest feeing—a feeling of self-pity. It was a bitter, fruitless, self-engrossing pity that he felt in that empty cottage, to the accompaniment of the hostile roar of the sea, spitting its spray to the very porch. Spitting and indifference and irksome noise, noise, noise—this appeared to be the basis of everything, the fundamental law of the world.

One night, after having lain with his thoughts and his pity for some time, he felt hungry. The Tartar and his wife slept in a room at the other end of the house. Stabesov took a candle and went to the cupboard in his underpants, the strings of which kept getting under his feet. There he found some bread, hard-boiled eggs and salt wrapped up in a piece of paper. He returned to his bed, and with his gaze fixed on the flame of the candle, peeled an egg and began to eat it slowly. Suddenly his eyes filled with tears. Nikolai Ivanovich hastily blew out the candle, pulled the covers up over his head and bit his lip as he repeated:

"Oh, hell, to hell with it all!"

Yekaterina Vasilievna had always had a weakness for peering through lighted windows when she was taking a walk. As she stood out on the snowy sidewalk, she was cut off from "those people" only by a thin pane of glass that muffled the sound. Yet "that" life seemed to her elusive and different. Here, for example, was a woman leaning on the arm of a chair, her chek on her hand. She was not even lost in thought, simply quiet. Her husband, collarless and in glasses, wetted his finger to turn the page of a book while his glance lingered on the green shade of the lamp. Or here, in a spotless half-basement room with a parquet floor sat three men—one at the piano, another moving a bow across the strings of the 'cello he held between his legs, and a third person sitting on a divan. And the expression on the face of this third person

171

was very serious, almost inspired. No sound was audible. The movements were slow and clumsy as though the people had become congealed for a brief instant without themselves realizing it and were listening to the flight of time whisking away the moments. Sad is man's face when left to himself!

Yekaterina Vasilievna wanted very much to glance through the lighted window of Stabesov's cottage, but she could not bring herself to do it. From the Tartar she had learned all the details of Nikolai Ivanovich's life, and concluded that he was "terrifically proud."

But one evening, as she was returning after dark from the sea, she made up her mind. Running up the path, she she stood on tiptoe and peeped into the window. Stabesov was standing in his vest, sewing a button on his coat by candle light.

"Heavens, the poor thing!" thought Yekaterina Vasilievna. The gravel crunched beneath her feet. Stabesov raised his head and looked through the window for a long time as Yekaterina Vasilievna hastened to her house.

When she arrived, she said to the nurse, "It's a dreadful thing, Maria Kapitonovna, when a man has no one to look after him. There is nothing sadder on earth."

To which the respected Maria Kapitnovna (who, as she herself maintained, knew men "inside out") answered disapprovingly, "Why waste pity on them?"

That evening Yekaterina Vasilievna felt particularly thankful that she had her home, her girls, and Maria Kapitonovna, "who loved the children as her own." And several times she sighed unconsciously on recalling how Stabesov had used the top of an inkwell instead of a thimble to push the needle.

On a slope among rugged pines bloomed a rhododendron bush. In one night it seemed to have burst into flame, so suddenly did its sturdy, artificial-looking flowers bloom forth. Stabesov caught sight of it from the window and went out into the garden. Yekaterina Vasilievna was sitting on a bench nearby. He bowed: she extended her hand and said that they

172

were acquainted. He was surprised by this kind, attentive way she looked at him with her long hazel eyes. It was as though she already knew something about him.

Nikolai Ivanovich smelled the bush, but the flowers had no scent. Yekaterina Vasilievna spoke of the bad spring and about the sea, finding it enchanting even on gloomy days. Stabesov considered a moment and agreed, then both of them turned and loked for some time at the agitated masses of water, the towering waves on the horizon.

Their meeting had been ordinary enough. It had even been a disappointment to Yekaterina Vasilievna, mainly because of Stabesov's tone, which she found too independent and self-sufficient ("And what about that button?" she thought). Nikolai Ivanovich, on the other hand, experienced a certain warmth in her presence, and his thoughts tended to be less hopeless that evening. The next day he suddenly found himself in need of writing paper, and he went over to Madame Bolotova's cottage, where he was, of course, made to stay for tea.

Yekaterina Vasilievna talked to him about her children, saying how much freedom they had here and how healthy it was for them; in a week each of them had gained half a pound, and their cheeks were like ripe peaches (when she spoke about her children, she made them seem as delicious as peaches); they were having difficulty with food supplies, but she was thinking of buying a goat; she also praised Maria Kapitonovna, who at that moment came in to get some hot water. As she drew it from the samovar into an enameled pot, the nurse cast a sidewise glance at the gentleman and pursed her wrinkled lips. "A rather mean lady," thought Stabesov. It was warm in the low room. The steam from the samovar cast shifting shadows on the ceiling where a long-legged spider was fly-hunting. In the nursery the little girls were relating some fantasies to each other. When she returned, Maria Kapitonovna muttered something and put them to bed. Stabesov played with his spoon, nodded his head, approved the purchase of the goat, made several attempts to cross his legs but was prevented by the low edge of the table, and all the while he kept thinking how pleasant all this was. Yekaterina Vasilievna accompanied him to the rhododendron bush which marked the boundary between their cottages; here they lingered a while, silently gazing into the darkness; then they prophesied good weather for the morrow and parted. For Stabesov, the rest of the evening and the night (half of which was sleepless) passed fairly decently—a bit wearisome, a bit lonely.

Two days later Yekaterina Vasilievna called on Stabesov for "something to read." Stabesov despairingly rummaged through his specialized books, papers and magazines.

"Here, this isn't so bad, more or less popular," he said, handing her a little grey booklet. Yekaterina Vasilievna rolled it up (it was evident that she was not much of a reader), perched herself on the window sill and began to chatter as she swung her foot against the wall.

She was wearing a soft navy blue dress which made her hands and neck seem amazingly delicate. On that day the sun was sometimes hidden behind heavy clouds, sometimes burst forth unexpectedly, burning into the wet earth and the sea, taking them by surprise, as it were, and hastened to chase away the shadows which were already scuttling about. And each time the light flared up outside the window, Yekaterina Vasilievna's hair was turned into old gold and the delicate shell of her ear became transparent.

As she discussed a play, which had recently created quite a stir in Moscow (Madame Bolotova was a great lover of the theater), she raised her hands and for some time adjusted the knot of hair on her neck. The taut sleeve gave a sharp outline to her elbow, and Nikolai Ivanovich, understanding little of what she was saying, began to be aware of her shoulder, her breast, and knee, under the soft material.

With every moment Yekaterina Vasilievna became less comprehensible, or rather she assumed a new mood which

174

could be comprehended only under the influence of something extraordinary, something out of the daily run. Her smile, the movement of her lips, the roguish shadows spreading from the corners of her mouth to her cheeks, her movements and her voice became unique and inimitable (he became very conscious of this quite suddenly). And all of this loveliness manifested itself when they were alone together, just the two of them.

This was a bit frightening, and a delightful little chill played strange music in his veins.

Evidently Yekaterina Vasilievna was also aware of something extraordinary. She blushed and seemed to say to Nikolai Ivanovich: "Here—this movement, this smile, this dimple, and this jest, are for you alone; they never belonged to anyone else, and never will."

Nikolai Ivanovich shook his head and said with a short laugh. "There's something I'd like to tell you—it's commonplace enough. I'm afraid you'd find it boring to listen to me."

He pulled a long face, but held his breath in expectation. Suddenly Yekaterina Vasilievna said in all seriousness:

"I am all attention."

"Everything is sheer deception, Yekaterina Vasilievna," he cried, sticking his thumbs into his vest pockets. "Even our most joyful moments are instantly blighted: can you think of anything more vicious than that? What the devil do I want with such moments if I have to die anyway? Here I am, thirty-two years old, which means I have only twenty years left—or rather twenty minutes! Is it possible to go on living like this? I keep hearing how time tears past like the wind on the roof. I feel like sitting down, clenching my teeth and waiting—for the end. It is painful to look at the sea, at the bright sky, at the flowers, at all those things that bind me to to the earth. Because all of it is sheer deception, and I'm not falling a victim to it. Look at my hand—a year ago it wasn't so wrinkled. That's the real truth for you, everything else is deception. Books, philosophy, art, humanism—the devil

175

take them all. I'm buried under a whole pyramid of such rubbish. I'm the most unhappy, the most degraded creature on earth, because—I have understood. And still I keep crawling out from under the heap like a worm in the rain."

Stabesov stopped and glanced into Yekaterina Vasilievna's unwinking eyes. She had even grown pale from strained attention. All the pity she had felt for this abandoned human being was permeated by his words. She did not doubt that he felt that way, but not for a minute did she believe that there was no escape from such despair. Scarcely restraining her tears, she took Nikolai Ivanovich by his hand (his fingers were ice-cold), and quickly, almost in a whisper, she said:

"You know that it is not true. Why do you speak like that? Remember, I have children; I couldn't possibly look upon them as dead."

He bent over her hand and kissed it several times. At every touch, his lips became warmer. He prolonged the last kiss for some time.

She saw his bent head with its thin, parted hair, she saw the collar which was too big for his neck, and she thought, "What a dear he is!"

"Now, you see!" she whispered.

Obviously these words were intended to say that no dead words could convince her that her child was born only to die, or that a person withered with loneliness was right in his views, or that the mind alone, unnourished by warm waves of feeling, could escape becoming dull and pathetic.

But she was incapable of saying all this, and only by a wonderful impulse (when she squeezed his hand and gazed into his eyes, repeating, "Now, you see?") did she bestow on Nikolai Ivanovich all her abundance of pity and tenderness.

It was much later that Stabesov understood this. Now he was conscious only that his horrible emptiness was being filled up with a warm and living beauty. He was so overcome by weakness that he went over to the divan and sat down.

"I have never said that to anyone else in my life," he said.

176

"And the strangest thing about it is that—yes, yes—apparently there must be another kind of truth. And you are—wonderfully wise. In one phrase you have refuted me more surely than could have been done in a thousand volumes."

(Later, neither he nor she could remember that strange phrase.)

Nikolai Ivanovich smiled as he lighted a cigarette. His eyes were shining. In her agitation and embarrassment, Yekaterina Vasilievna suddenly remembered that it was time to feed the children, and went home. When she had gone, Stabesov stretched out on the divan and continued to smoke and smile.

That was how their friendship began.

The days became warmer and more enchanting. The grapevine on the southern slope grew green; the sticky leaves of the hedges had curled up; the evening air was filled with the scent of flowers and the sea.

Masses of bright clouds rose above the mountains and stood motionless in the sky until sunset. The sea reflected the clouds and the gulls.

Stabesov and Yekaterina Vasilievna were always together, sometimes on the sands where the children were playing, sometimes in the mountains where they went in search of wild asparagus which grew in ditches among thorn bushes. After their search, they would lie on a blanket and look down from the heights upon the vast expanse of water patterned with blue where the currents crossed and at the dense cloud banks beyond the promontory.

It seemed as though far, far away, there stood a sacrificial altar from which huge clouds of smoke were rising. This did not reveal very subtle imagination, but they liked the idea, and repeated it every time they glanced at the sky.

In a few days the health of Nikolai Ivanovich showed marked improvement. He became bright, energetic, and witty. He described the dullnesss of his former life by quoting books —so closely had his past been bound up with books and images of other men's creating.

"I was the most ordinary kind of bookworm," he told her now. "An intellectual who was mortally afraid of fresh air, I could not even imagine the joy of resting and looking at the clouds. Something has happened—something has happened—"

Yekaterina Vasilievna, completely in the grip of their friendship, grew more thoughtful and prettier than ever before. Her face was delicately tanned. She thought of Stabesov all the time—tenderly, anxiously, and with some perplexity. Sometimes, as she lay in bed, she would cry. But she could not have explained what it was that caused her alarm, what premonitions clouded her joy. And the more simple, friendly, and cheerful Nikolai Ivanovich was in her company, the more upset she became at the end of each long, sparkling, joyful day.

Little crabs as quick as spiders appeared among the rocks. The children splashed barefoot through the lazy tide in an effort to catch them, but the crabs were too nimble for them.

Nikolai Ivanovich lay stretched out on the sand. Only the end of his nose, his smiling mouth and his beard could be seen under the edge of his hat. As Yekaterina Vasilievna watched the children, her heart beat faster, so delightful was the splashing of the water, the smell of the sea breeze, the sun, the high voices of the children in their white, knee-length dresses.

The girls had no luck with the crabs, and they cried, "Mamma, come help us!" Yekaterina Vasilievna threw off her sand-filled slippers, took off her stockings, gathered up the skirt of her white dress and entered the water, laughing merrily at her fear. A moist coolness lapped gently at her feet. Behind a stone hid a large crab with tragic, bulging eyes. She quickly reached down for it, but the crab slipped away and disappeared in the muddied water. In the enthusiasm of pursuit, she kept going further, splashing through the waves and wetting the sleeves and the hem of her dress. But she managed to catch one little crab, which wriggled about, tickling the palm of her hand.

178

"Just look how hideous it is!" she exclaimed, coming out of the water.

Stabesov, raising himself on his elbow, stared at her as though seeing her for the first time. Her heart sank.

"How awkward, how stupid!" she thought, hastily letting down her skirt. She sat down on the sand and sought protection behind her parasol, blushing until the tears came.

The children took the crab and ran off with it, far along the edge of the water.

Stabesov turned over on the sand and said, drawing out his words, "I was thinking as I watched you: the poets once called woman a perfect creation of nature. That is, of course, a commonplace, but still it contains a measure of truth (that is how he expressed it: "a measure of truth"). When a woman appears on the landscape, a change immediately takes place in nature: for the spectator, what had been pure contemplation becomes, if I may say so, provoking. It acts on the nerves, rousing entirely different emotions."

Suddenly he laughed, revealing a gold tooth in the back corner of his mouth. Then he hastily added:

"Of course, I am joking, my dear Yekaterina Vasilievna."

Without answering, Yekaterina Vasilievna drew her bare feet under her dress in horror. And when Stabesov pulled at her parasol to get a look at her face, she cried angrily "Leave me alone!" and, gathering up her slippers and stockings, she ran away.

They did not see each other that evening. On the next day Stabesov spoke seriously with Yekaterina Vasilievna, blaming yesterday's jest on his own clumsiness, embarrassment, etc. Everything was patched up, of course, and they did not again refer to the unpleasantness.

Nikolai Ivanovich was sitting on the same steps where a month before he had sat and frowned at the wind and the salt spray. Now the sea was only slightly disturbed and the crest of each wave was tinged with blue; the entire expanse of the water was sun-spangled, and it seemed that it must have been on just such a day that Icarus, in the intoxication of ecstasy, had fastened his wings with wax and soared above the sea towards the sun, the source of all life.

Yekaterina Vasilievna came up behind him and said:

"Look, a sail."

The black silhouette of a boat carrying a diagonal Tartar sail slid shorewards at a sharp incline over the dazzling surface of the sea.

Nikolai Ivanovich said, "One could sit here for hours absorbing this eternal life through one's eyes and ears and very pores. I can understand the kingdom of heaven on earth: one should achieve immortality here, in this world. Every moment becomes an eternity in my emotional experience."

Yekaterina Vasilievna sat down next to him on the step, leaned her elbows on her knees, and dropped her chin on her fists. During the three days since the incident with the crab her face had assumed a new severity, as though she had been immersed in a cold bath. She either avoided long conversations with Nikolai Ivanovich or else listened absent-mindedly. For a long time he studied her graceful profile with a sprinkling of freckles that gave her a girlish look.

"However funny it may sound, the fact is that I'm a little bit afraid of you," he said. "If it weren't for that ridiculous fear, I'd tell you something."

She shook her head in annoyance and continued to gaze at the approaching sail. Nikolai Ivanovich gave a short laugh:

"What I want to say is connected with my whole perception of life. I shall have to say it sometime: it is of tremendous importance to me."

Yekaterina Vasilievna suddenly interrupted him, still without turning her head:

"You're an egoist—the most complete egoist I've ever known in my life." Her voice was sharp. "Not even an egoist— just an absurd bookworm."

In utter amazement, Nikolai Ivanovich asked what she could mean. Receiving no answer, he shrugged his shoulders

180

and pretended to be offended. Gradually his hands began to tremble.

In a few minutes Yekaterina Vasilievna said cheerfully.

"Now I know whose boat that is. It belongs to the brother of your watchman, the Tartar Mamai-khan, though of course he's no khan at all, but just a fisherman. Let's go for a sail."

She rose quickly and ran down to the sea. Nikolai Ivanovich watched her graceful step and the way her white batiste dress blew in the wind. She spoke to the fisherman, then turned round and beckoned to him. "How do you like that?" muttered Nikolai Ivanovich to himself. "First I'm an egoist, then—oh, for the love of God!" and he climbed down, hanging on to the railing.

Mamai-khan grinned on seeing him, placed a board from the bow to the shore, and helped them climb in.

At first it was necessary to row away from shore. Then the sail was hoisted, the boat careened, and frothing waves broke against the bow.

Mamai-khan sat at the rudder, with his sheepskin hat pushed to the back of his head. His quilted pants were rolled up to the knees of his sinuous legs; a copper chain holding amulets was strung through his vest; his pock-marked, sun-blackened face remained indifferent to all the vicissitudes of life. Whenever the wind grew stronger, filling the sails until the mast creaked, he bared his white teeth and spat in the sea. It was said that before the war Mamai-khan had carried contraband goods from Constantinople in this boat—tobacco, silk, and weapons. He was a son of this rocky, seawashed earth, an earth now in full bloom and careless of death, an earth which Stabesov now really saw for the first time.

Nikolai Ivanovich toyed with his beard. He had a passing sense of being hurt, as though he had not been invited to join in a game. He had been called an egoist. But again the proximity of Yekaterina Vasilievna made him forget all these complications.

She had flung herself face down in the bow of the boat, her

181

white-stockinged legs crossed, her tousled head propped up, gazing meditatively at the waves. Two buttons had come unfastened on the back of her dress near the neck, where the sunburn ended. "What a vulgar imagination I have after all!" thought Stabesov. Then he lay down beside her and said, "Well?" Naturally, she did not answer. His desire was absolutely clear: to bend down and kiss her on the lips. His mind was in a turmoil. Stabesov leaned on his elbow and plucked at his beard. Low over the water swooped a gull; a particularly large wave struck the bow, covering them with refreshing spray. And it seemed that the wave was soft-scented, as were the sea and the sail and the wind—all of them were laden with the warm scent of carnation emanating from Yekaterina Vasilievna's dress and hair.

"You're a darling, a real darling," said Stabesov in a strained voice.

Yekaterina Vasilievna's shoulder twitched—and nothing more.

He took her hand and touched it with his cold nose, straining to kiss her cheek, which was also fragrant with carnation. Yekaterina Vasilievna freed her hand and continued silently gazing at the waves. He noticed that her eyes were filled with tears.

Nikolai Ivanovich lighted two candles in the candlesticks on the table and placed two others on the washstand to make the room brighter and more festive. He drew the curtain and he himself covered the tea table with a clean sheet in lieu of a tablecloth. He found some marmelade and cakes in a suitcase. The Tartar brought in the samovar and put the lid on.

With an appraising glance at the room, Nikolai Ivanovich began to walk back and forth, stopping to light a cigarette; with his thin legs, he paced diagonally across the unpainted floor, listening for the slightest sound, laughing softly to himself, adjusting a lock of hair that fell into his eyes.

He was wearing a clean collar and a black soft bow tie. He had taken off his pince-nez and placed them on the inkwell.

182

To his nearsighted eyes the flames of the candles were misty yellow spots, as though seen through the steam of a bathhouse. But he knew that his eyes were far more expressive without his glasses.

Earlier in the day, while they were still in the boat after his unsuccessful attempt to kiss her, Stabesov had invited Yekaterina Vasilievna "to have a cup of tea with him this evening." She had answered shortly, "I'll come." Nothing else of any importance had transpired in the boat.

Now it was late; apparently Yekaterina Vasilievna was putting the children to bed and, at any moment, she would rap on the window.

The purpose of this invitation was: "to spend an evening in friendly conversation." That was how Nikolai Ivanovich formulated it—making, perhaps, the mental reservation that certain liberties might be allowed if they developed out of the conversation. But no more than this. He consciously suppressed ideas of going any "further," for "he had never been a boor," and considered it demeaning to lure a woman with the aid of tea and marmelade.

And yet, at present, he found all his preparations distasteful. He was ashamed of the marmelade, and especially of the fact that he had taken off his pince-nez. "But one can't always be expected to be up to the mark," he thought, washing his hands with eau-de-Cologne.

He did not doubt for a moment that Yekaterina Vasilievna would come. In general, Stabesov could not imagine her without himself; whenever he thought of her, he was present; his imagination never accompanied her to the house with the tiled roof; when she left him, it was as though she disappeared altogether; but her words, her smile, her movements and fragrance, all her unspeakable loveliness rose in his memory with exhausting frequency, agitating him with ever new poignancy.

The clock struck nine. Nikolai Ivanovich stopped abruptly and glanced into the darkness of the next room where the clock was ticking. Then he pushed back the curtains and

183

glanced through the window. He was conscious of the softly beating surf, the perfume of flowers and the sea. All the lights were out in the cottage. "Strange," he muttered, feeling his heart race, then sink. He put on his pince-nez and went out.

The brief sunset had long since faded from the sky, but the night had not yet lighted all its stars or taken complete possession. On the steps at the embankment he made out the vague whiteness of a seated figure. Nikolai Ivanovich approached. She quickly turned her head as though upset—or perhaps it only seemed so to him.

"So this is where you are," he said softly. "And here I was waiting for you. The samovar cooled off long ago."

With a glance into his face, she slowly reached out for the railing and got up. She had just been crying bitterly over the fact that Nikolai Ivanovich had reduced all the excitement and complications of their relationship to a cup of tea, and that she had agreed to go, and that she would certainly go and drink that bitter cup, and that at the moment she was sitting by the dark, eternal sea, which would continue to murmur in just the same way after she was dead and after everybody else was dead.

On hearing footsteps, she had almost jumped up and run away. Nikolai Ivanovich stopped at her side and muttered something in a hoarse, agitated voice. Her heart sank. She glanced penetratingly at this man whose eyes were hidden behind pince-nez in which the stars were reflected. And suddenly it seemed to her that he was doomed to die that very year—thin, lonely, pathetic—and that the fact of his inviting her to drink tea with him was obvious and pitiful subtlety. The moment had come when the stern angel abandoned her post. The most meagre words of love would have been enough for Yekaterina Vasilievna. Let him only knock, however softly and tenderly, and the gates would be joyfully thrown open.

"Now he will take my hand and say, 'My darling, my life, I love you,'" thought Yekaterina Vasilievna, "and I will give myself to him entirely, remaining true to him, to myself, and to my children."

She hung her head and was silent. Her hand slipped from the railing and fell at her side. But at that moment Nikolai Ivanovich was exerting all his energy to formulate phrases which should express the innocence of his intentions. His tongue clung to the roof of his mouth. Silence was fatal. He felt that, but was powerless, for he did not understand what was taking place. The moment passed.

Suddenly Yekaterina Vasilievna asked in a trembling, almost severe voice,

"Nikolai Ivanovich, do you love me?"

He moved toward her, breathing heavily, and took her hand. "How can you ask me? I can no longer sleep at night. I think of you all the time. My emotions have made a sick man of me. Tonight I waited for you like a crazy man. . . . Why do you behave so strangely with me? I realize how clumsy I am, but everything is on fire within me. You torture me, and you do not wish to understand. . . ."

"But do you love me?" she interrupted.

He dropped her hand, which fell inanimately and wiped his brow. Yekaterina Vasilievna began to laugh quietly.

"You are capable of smothering any feeling," muttered Nikolai Ivanovich. "You breathe the coldness of a cellar."

She took him by the arm and drew him toward the cottage, saying with the same laughter:

"My dear friend, difficult conversations should be carried on in the darkness, where you can't see each other's eyes and feel ashamed. Then it is possible to come to the point. I only asked you if you loved me—a perfectly innocent question, but you immediately became angry. You and I are very bad lovers, but we shall be very good friends. Now let's go to your house and have tea."

Yekaterina Vasilievna laughed out loud when they entered the room and she noticed the candles on the washstand, the sheet, and all the details. Then she sat down at the samovar

185

and acted as hostess, calling Stabesov a "miserable bachelor."
He sat with a crooked, frozen smile on his face and gave the
wrong answers. He was hurt, wounded, agitated, perplexed. . . .
In the end, he became indignant:

"I am forced to realize that you consider me a vulgar beast,"
he said, glancing with repulsion at his thin hands. "That
is how you interpret my behavior. But that is nonsense, a
lie. You have upset me. You can't act like that toward—
toward—" he twisted his beard in his fury "—toward one
who loves you. Yes, I'm in love with you!"

Yekaterina Vasilievna sat down beside him on the divan,
drew in her feet and covered them with her skirt.

"So that's how you declare your love! It would be better
if I didn't understand Russian," she said, and threw back her
head on the cushions. "Perhaps it would be better for us to say
nothing."

Stabesov snorted, pulled out an empty match box and
hurled it at the wall, yanked at his vest, fumed, calmed down,
and finally glanced at Yekaterina Vasilievna out of the corner
of his eye. She was sitting sad and lovely with her head thrown
back. There was not the slightest shadow of ridicule on her
delicate lips. After a moment's pause she said in a scarcely
audible voice:

"Well, we have patched it up."

As he gazed at her face, he again became conscious of the
warm scent of carnation. Softly and uncertainly he touched
her hand.

"It's all so sad," she whispered.

"What is?"

She did not answer, and he began to draw his own conclu-
sions. "Oh, yes, I understand," he thought. "What you need is
a handsome brute who will grab you by those hands, twisting
and torturing you. . . . You find it sad that I have not the
muscles of an ox. . . ."

"Oh, how sad it is," she repeated with a sudden sigh, and
he saw that her lips were trembling.

186

Stabesov got up and kissed her lips clumsily and painfully. Suddenly a wild look entered her long, amazed eyes.

"Listen, listen," muttered Stabesov, grabbing her by the shoulders. . . .

Her agitated voice mingled with his hoarse muttering. The green bolster rolled off the divan to the floor. At last Yekaterina Vasilievna tore herself free from his hands, jumped up, and walked over to the table. . . . Her flushed face seemed suddenly to have become thin. She looked long and furiously at Stabesov with clear, cold eyes. . . . Never before had she seemed so lovely.

"You're a fool," she said in a ringing voice. "You're simply loathsome, and I'll never forgive you this insult."

Suddenly she closed her eyes tightly and huge tears welled from beneath her lashes. Then she rushed toward the door and, turning around, all aflame with anger:

"You won't forget that you have offended me!"

"I'm wretchedly unhappy," said Stabesov in a dull voice which he himself could not hear. "Don't go away. Have pity on me."

Then she gathered up her skirts and nodded her disheveled head.

"I hate you now. Now we shall never see each other again."

And she left. For some time he stood listening to the crunching of the gravel. Then he felt in his vest pocket for his pince-nez and went out to the embankment.

The heavens burned with the blue fire of the constellations and, far out on the horizon, the Milky Way was reflected in the dark waters of the sea.

Stabesov sat on the steps and held his chin in his hands. . . . In the darkness the earth was invisible. Here he was utterly alone. The earth seemed to have flown away to the stars, and an inscrutable expanse of ether separated him from this earth, from this life which, for such a brief instant, had lured him with warmth and beauty.